Home Visits Library Service
Mitcham Library. 157. London Road, Mitcham, Surrey CR4 2YR
Telephone Answer Machine 0208 274 5910

PRITTY		
GRICA		

An Absence of Angels

Also by Janie Bolitho

Kindness can Kill (1993)
Ripe for Revenge (1994)
Motive for Murder (1994)
Dangerous Deceit (1995)
Finger of Fate (1996)
Sequence of Shame (1996)
Snapped in Cornwall (1997)

AN ABSENCE OF ANGELS

Janie Bolitho

Constable · London

First published in Great Britain 1997
by Constable & Company Ltd
3 The Lanchesters, 162 Fulham Palace Road
London W6 9ER
Copyright © 1997 by Janie Bolitho
The right of Janie Bolitho to be
identified as the author of this work
has been asserted by her in accordance
with the Copyright, Designs and Patents Act 1988
ISBN 0 09 477350 3
Set in Linotron Palatino 10 pt by
Pure Tech India Ltd
Printed and bound in Great Britain by
Hartnolls Limited, Bodmin, Cornwall

A CIP catalogue record for this book
is available from the British Library.

For Dylan, my brother

1

Owen Kerslake was looking forward to a bath and a meal. Every muscle ached and he was pleasantly tired. After the dark winter months and a dearth of work he felt light-hearted as he descended his ladder, secured the lid of the paint pot and carried the paraphernalia of his trade to the back of his van.

The evening was balmy and warm. Because the nights were pulling out Owen had worked until dusk, anxious to get on with the job as he had several more lined up and he wanted to make up the financial shortfall which had occurred since Christmas. He looked up at the gleaming white walls and the shiny black woodwork, satisfied with what he had accomplished and pleased that the occupants had chosen the most appropriate colour scheme for the gabled building with its wide angled roof which sloped gracefully to the sides of the property.

Traffic was lighter now and once he was on the main road he was able to complete the journey home in less than ten minutes.

The van was kept overnight in one of the lock-ups in a row of garages. A couple of the up-and-over doors were in good repair, some were scrawled with graffiti and his own was rusting, the paint flaking to reveal grey aluminium. He smiled. He was no different from a lot of men. Dee was always on at him about the state of the house but just as solicitors fail to draw up their own wills and plumbers never get around to replacing the washers in their own dripping taps, the idea of decorating his own house was anathema.

He whistled as he walked down the narrow path between the garages. A group of boys were kicking a ball against one of the doors; each direct hit clanged and reverberated through the quiet evening air but a blackbird, unperturbed, continued singing in the boughs of a flowering sycamore.

The council houses were built on a slope and overlooked Rickenham Green. From the upstairs windows of many of

5

them the spire of St Luke's church could be seen. It now stood amongst supermarkets and building societies, a rare historical reminder of the original hamlet and therefore safely under the aegis of conservationists. Visitors came to study the ancient headstones in the small graveyard.

Owen rounded the corner and entered one of the rows containing identical red-brick properties, each with a small patch of garden, most with a car outside. Here, more children played in the road: three girls, two holding a rope, chanted, as the third skipped; another sat on the kerb engrossed in a miniature video game. Two youths on skateboards almost ran him down as he crossed the street. Soon their mothers would call them in and all would be quiet. Owen wondered if there was any beer in the fridge.

The only lock on the front door was an ordinary Yale but they were lucky because there were few break-ins on the estate. Owen joked that it was because it was peopled by half the criminal fraternity of the town. 'They don't shit on their own doorstep,' he was fond of commenting. And the neighbours all knew one another and spent a great deal of time minding everyone else's business instead of their own.

He turned the key. 'Dee?' The house was unusually silent, there were no muted television sounds, no crackling radio. Wherever she was she would be home soon. Since they got together three years ago he had helped her to establish a routine. Apart from weekends they ate somewhere between seven and eight o'clock.

Owen had removed his paint-spattered overalls in the garage. His shoes were dusty, his jeans frayed, and there was a hole under the arm of his T-shirt where the stitching was coming undone. These were his working clothes but every night he changed out of them before they sat down to eat.

Upstairs he put the plug in the bath and ran the taps. Dee had not said she was going out; perhaps her mother wasn't well. He yanked off his T-shirt and flung it on the floor then added a generous measure of Radox to the water. Pine-perfumed steam filled the air. Something had briefly flitted through his mind as he had mounted the stairs. He had un-

6

buckled his belt before he realised what it was. The kitchen door was closed. They never shut it: Dee liked to hear the television or call out to him as she got their meal. The water had turned aquamarine. Owen turned off the taps.

Downstairs, for some inexplicable reason, he glanced into the living-room first. Nothing had altered. It was tidy: Dee's magazine on the cushion of the settee; the waste bin empty; the carpet vacuumed. On the windowsill a bunch of freesias stood in a glass, their thin stems rigid, the scent of their petals heady, almost sickly.

Owen left the room. The stairs were on his left, running up the side of the house; the kitchen was behind the living-room. He opened the door and stared blankly at the carnage. For several seconds the scene was incomprehensible. He gagged. Sinking to his knees he clutched his stomach with one hand and the smoothness of the Bakelite door knob with the other.

Dee was sprawled on the floor in a congealing pool of blood. Her clothes were soaked in it, her shaggy blonde hair was black and sticky. He tried not to look but his eyes were drawn back. Pink speckles reached as high as the ceiling, there was blood on the kettle and a smeared hand mark on the wall, yet what revolted him most was the cubes of raw beef on the chopping board. This time he vomited.

When the heaving had stopped he crawled to the foot of the stairs and sat on the bottom one. Quite impassively he noticed that there was blood on his shoe and on the pale carpet where he had walked. Finally, after five or fifty minutes, he did not know, he staggered to the telephone which was on a table by the living-room door. Replacing the receiver he opened the front door and waited. When the police arrived they found him on the settee with one of Dee's magazines in his hands.

At Rickenham Green headquarters Owen Kerslake was cautioned a second time because it was abundantly clear that he had been too dazed to understand the words previously.

He was questioned extensively, the same questions and the same answers being thrown back and forth. He had been at work, his employers could vouch for him, apart from his

7

lunch hour. The kitchen knife might or might not have been their own, he did not know. Nor could he say why there were no fingerprints on it. He simply did not know and he was foolish enough to add that he did not care. His life was in ruins. On and on it went. Where had he hidden the clothes he must have changed out of? Where was the towel he had used after a shower? He tried to tell the truth but there was a fog in his brain. When he remembered something or changed a statement he had already made it sounded feeble even to his own ears. He spent the night in the care of the Rickenham Green police but as there was nowhere else for him to go it did not matter. Men were still at the house going through their possessions and he knew he could never set foot in it again. He could not bring himself to ask what they had done with Dee.

The following morning he made a brief appearance in court to be charged with murder. Bail was not granted. Owen had no relatives, no responsible person into whose care he could be discharged, and the seriousness of the crime was against him. He was removed to prison in a police van where he was to remain on remand awaiting trial. It might take months.

As far as the press were concerned the case had become *sub judice* and therefore they were forbidden to mention the events of six years previously when Owen Kerslake had also been under suspicion.

2

Detective Chief Inspector Ian Roper had promised to spend the weekend with his wife at her mother's house down on the coast. He was not about to break that promise, there had been too much of that in the past. Had he been on duty Moira would have gone alone. Ian liked Aldeburgh and was looking forward to the trip apart from the cloud of uncertainty which hung over him.

'Have a good weekend,' Superintendent Thorne told him. 'And, Ian, it's done with, okay?'

Ian nodded, gave Mike Thorne a fleeting smile and carried his briefcase out to the car.

Friday night, and the first evening since the previous autumn when he had not left headquarters in darkness. After the long winter it was a surprise to walk out into the warm air. The raised flowerbeds were now filled with poly-anthus plants. The tulip petals were fully open and about to drop; the rose bushes had sprouted leaves. None of this lifted Ian's mood. He drove across town with a scowl on his face.

Moira had taken the afternoon off in order to pack for them both. As soon as he had had a cup of tea and a change of clothes they would be leaving. It was such a short journey they could have driven there and back each day but it was not the same as staying with someone for the weekend and, he admitted wryly, his ready co-operation in agreeing to occupy Philippa Lawrence's spare bedroom had a lot to do with the fact that he would be free to indulge in as many pints of Adnam's bitter as he wanted. It was officially his weekend off; there would be no interruptions from his bleeper or mobile phone.

He was earlier than usual so when he pulled into Belmont Terrace he found a parking space directly outside number 14. As he locked the car he recalled that Owen Kerslake had as good as admitted his guilt and that the evidence against him was far more than circumstantial. There was also the question of his past, although the jury would know nothing of that. But even a convincing confession is not proof of guilt and Ker-slake's did not fall into that category.

Moira heard his key in the lock and met him in the hall where he almost fell over the hold-all which stood ready. Automatically he slid his briefcase into the space under the telephone table and bent to kiss his wife. He had to bend: at five feet four inches she was a foot shorter than him. She was wearing flat canvas shoes, light blue jeans and a thin pullover, and the fifteen years' discrepancy in their ages was more than apparent. He ruffled her fair, shoulder-length hair. Unknown

9

to him its colour was now enhanced artificially. 'Give me five minutes, then we'll make a move.'

'That's fine. I'm ready anyway. Do you want some tea first?'

'I'd love a cup. I'll just have a quick wash while you make it. Where're my beige trousers?' he shouted from the bedroom.

'On a hanger in the wardrobe,' she called back over the noise of the water filling the kettle. Where they always are, and they're not beige, they're fawn, she added silently. She was used to Ian's absent-mindedness and his inability to find something even if it was under his nose. At work he was quite a different man and she knew that he relied upon her more than he would care to admit when it came to domestic matters.

It had surprised Moira that Ian had so readily agreed to accompany her but it was time he had a proper break. More surprising was the fact that he was missing the opportunity of watching one of the last Norwich City home games. The season was almost over. She guessed that he was unhappy with the outcome of his latest case but, unusually, he was reluctant to discuss it with her. The next two days would allow him some breathing space, some time to think through what was bothering him and to put it in perspective.

'Which one's mine?' Ian picked up the mug which Moira pushed towards him. He was casually dressed in the fawn trousers and an open-necked shirt. It was not yet summer and Moira thought he was being optimistic but wisely made no comment as she added sweeteners to her own tea.

'How's Barry doing? I keep meaning to ring Lucy but I haven't got around to it.'

'And you say I'm always talking shop.' Ian shrugged. 'He doesn't say much but he should be all right.'

Moira emptied the pot, rinsed out the mugs and left them upside down on the draining board. Lucy Swan had become a good friend. Her husband, Barry, was a detective sergeant but was studying for his inspector's exams. Both the Swans had been subdued since Lucy's miscarriage but they were gradually coming to terms with it. Moira found it strange that there was a chance her friend might have young children

10

about the same time as she and Ian became grandparents. Not that there were any signs of that happening yet. Their son, Mark, was in his final year at art college and was temporarily without a girlfriend. 'I'm playing the field, Mother,' he had told her the last time he telephoned. She was not sure how many tears this had caused or why he had started addressing her as Mother.

'Come on then, don't stand there day-dreaming.'

Moira was unaware that she had been gazing out of the window without seeing the back garden to which she devoted so much time and effort. With a cursory glance at the spring flowers she followed Ian out to the car.

Moira's question reminded Ian that if Barry was successful he might lose him. They had worked together for a number of years: worked, as many did not, in tandem. And who would be made up to sergeant in his stead? Not DC Campbell. He was steady and reliable and thorough but would never rise above his present rank. Markham already held the rank and, as far as anyone knew, had no intention of going higher, but where Markham was concerned how much did anyone know? 'We could do a lot worse than Brenda Gibbons.'

'Pardon?'

'Sorry. Thinking aloud.'

Moira shrugged and settled back to watching the scenery. The hedgerows were thickening and the grass was a rich green. Nature had soon restored it after the parched months of the previous summer.

In less than an hour they reached their destination. Philippa Lawrence heard the car and came out to welcome them. Each time Ian saw her he was struck by the resemblance between mother and daughter. Both were fine-boned and slender, and they were very much alike facially although Philippa wore her hair cut short and feathered. With a jolt he realised he was nearer his mother-in-law's age than his wife's.

Kisses and hugs were exchanged. 'It's a shame about the weather.' Philippa looked uncertainly at the sky. A sea fret was closing in from the horizon. 'It was such a beautiful day, now this. Anyway, it's lovely to see you both.'

They trooped into the stone cottage, one behind the other as the passageway was narrow. Ian had to stoop beneath the lintels. He liked Philippa; she was intelligent and a good listener, but further in her favour was her disregard of adverse propaganda when it came to food. From her kitchen came red meat, pies and puddings and there was always proper butter for the toast. No criticism of Moira was implied because she tried to keep the the incipient bulge over his belt under control. He was unable to do so himself.

'I expect you're ready for a drink. I've got almost everything here but we can go to the pub if you prefer?' The question was directed at Ian.

'No, I'd rather unwind here.' Normally he would have preferred the latter suggestion but he was bone tired and it would be nice to spend an hour listening to the two women talk, catching up on gossip.

Philippa poured beer and two glasses of white wine. 'It was so warm earlier that I only prepared a salad for supper.' She met Moira's eyes and they both smiled. Ian's face had dropped. 'I did make a chicken and ham pie to go with it, though.'

'Ah, great.' Ian wondered why they were laughing.

As they ate he found he was physically beginning to relax; he could almost feel the tension draining away. Philippa noticed the gradual change in his demeanour and was only being tactful when she asked if he had been particularly busy recently. Their conversation so far had selfishly concerned herself and Moira. 'It must get you down dreadfully at times,' she added, not having seen Moira's slight shake of the head.

'It does sometimes. And you'll have heard about this latest fiasco.'

'Fiasco?'

'Ian doesn't believe the man they've arrested is guilty,' Moira clarified, hoping her assessment of the cause of his anxiety was correct.

'Good heavens, don't you? Still, that's for a jury to decide now, isn't it?'

'Sadly, yes. And everything points to his guilt.' Ian stopped.

He ought not to discuss Owen Kerslake or the case before the trial – or afterwards, to be strictly pedantic.

'Come on, Ian, you know Mum wouldn't dream of repeating anything you say.'

He nodded. 'I do, but it's not that. I honestly want to forget about it.'

Philippa made sure the subject was dropped by going out to the kitchen to make coffee.

Sleep did not come easily to Ian that night. Moira's eyes were closed almost immediately, but she had spent many nights in her mother's spare room. It was not just the unfamiliarity of his surroundings; Ian needed to rationalise his thoughts, to see if he could find any reasonable explanation for why he believed Kerslake to be innocent. There was so much against him. He was closest to the victim, he had claimed to find the body, he had no provable alibi for his lunch hour, no one had seen anyone enter the house, there were no unaccounted-for fingerprints, and the knife with which Dee Mercer had been killed was found at the scene, washed clean of blood and fingerprints in the sink. And Kerslake had confessed. According to the pathologist the woman had died quickly: the first couple of blows would have been enough, the other wounds were inflicted after death. There were no signs of a struggle and no signs of a forced entry, therefore either Dee had admitted her killer or he or she had been in possession of a key. Dee had been easily overpowered, which suggested her attacker was a male. Ian had to accept that everything pointed towards Kerslake's guilt. Unless she had been taken by surprise.

Kerslake had stated that he had gone to the park between one and two o'clock, something he did regularly if the weather permitted. He sat on a bench and read the paper whilst he ate his sandwiches and drank tea from his flask. It had been dry on the day of the murder, with a fresh wind, but Kerslake's bench had been in a sheltered position.

The park was a ten-minute drive from the house upon which he had been working, as was his own house. He was seen driving off a little after one and he had returned at five past two but no one had come forward to say they had noticed

13

his van anywhere in the vicinity of the park gates. In his favour was a lack of witnesses to place the van near his own property during that hour – but not many people were around, and the groups of children who often gathered in the streets and around the garages would at that time have been in school.

Ian sighed and turned over but was unable to find a comfortable position. He swore under his breath. Owen Kerslake's face floated before his eyes. Forensic evidence had been inconclusive but showed no signs of a stranger having been in the house. Neighbours had been questioned but no one had noticed any unusual vehicles or people they did not know on the relevant day. Dee's own mother had been too ill to talk. On and on it went . . . Ian's mind raced as he dredged up all the facts he could remember.

Unlike many people, Dee Mercer put her diary to good use. The hours she worked part-time in a fish and chip shop were carefully recorded, possibly to ensure she was not underpaid. There was a note of two dental appointments and one with a hairdresser where she had also added the stylist's name. Several entries simply stated 'Mum' with a time against each. There were other names, all female, each of whom had confirmed that they had met Dee on those occasions for shopping or coffee. He just doesn't strike me as a murderer, Ian thought, although he could not have said who would. No, it's just that I don't see him as one, he amended, aware of the subtle difference.

In the small hours he finally slept.

The following two days passed without a mention of Kerslake or Dee Mercer. On Saturday morning the three of them went for a long walk then Ian insisted on buying them a pub lunch. Later they sat on the beach beneath the wall which acted as a windbreak and enjoyed the warmth of the April sun.

'Oh, no, Ian, you mustn't,' Philippa protested after they had returned to the cottage to shower. He had told her he had reserved a table for dinner. 'You oughtn't to spoil me, I'll get too used to it.'

'You're entitled to a day off,' he said and the matter was

14

settled. 'But I shall be rewarded no doubt?' He smiled charmingly.

'Ah, I expect you're referring to roast pork with crackling. I know you've seen it in the fridge, with home-made herb stuffing and apple sauce and plenty of vegetables. Am I right?'

'Indeed you are. Dare I ask if we'll be having pudding?'

'If you've room. Treacle tart and cream.'

'Oh, honestly, Mother. How will I cope next week?' Moira laughed but it was not so much at the delight on Ian's face as at the way in which she had unwittingly copied Mark's form of address. 'Mother', then, was used to express disapproval mixed with resigned affection.

It was Moira who drove them back on Sunday evening. Ian was slumped in the front seat, arms folded, head swaying in time to the motion of the car as he snored gently. Moira ignored it, it could have been worse. On top of several pints of Adnam's he had had two helpings of pork and was unable to refuse Philippa's treacle tart. Moira concentrated on the traffic as they neared Rickenham Green. Many other trippers were returning home at the same time.

'Ian, you mustn't brood on it,' she told him as they got ready for bed. 'It's out of your hands now.'

'I know.' Mike Thorne had said much the same thing but Ian suspected that Mike, too, had his own ideas about the case. He was proved right the following day.

3

'Moira was asking after you.' Ian had met Barry on the stairs.

'As women frequently do.' DS Barry Swan smirked. Except that his womanising days were over. Since he had first met Lucy he had been hooked, fascinated by her independence and her ability to run her own life. She was the antidote to the females whom he had kept waiting or stood up and who still came back for more.

15

'I was referring to the studying, actually. How's it going?'

'So, so.' His tone implied it was going less than well.

'Any news on Dee Mercer's daughter yet? Has she turned up?'

'Not that I know of. I wasn't in yesterday. Oh, the Super wants a word in your shell-like.'

'When?' Ian hoped his optimism was not misplaced. Surely Thorne had his doubts too?

'Some time this morning.'

They had reached Ian's office. He nodded vaguely in the direction of the internal telephone. 'Find out when exactly, would you?' Whilst Barry spoke to Thorne's secretary Ian ran over the little they knew of Kelly Mercer. She had left home at sixteen but the circumstances surrounding her departure were vague. She had not been heard of since. No one had reported her missing so it had to be assumed that her mother was happy for her to be wherever she was. Yet there had been no correspondence in the house nor was a telephone number for Kelly listed. Ian did not think this was particularly odd. Most mothers would not need to keep a note of their daughter's number.

All the neighbours had been able to come up with was the fact that Kelly's leaving had roughly coincided with the advent of Owen Kerslake on the scene.

All forms of media had covered the murder yet Kelly had not come forward. Ian wondered if she would appear at the funeral.

If there had been a family row it had been severe enough to cause a complete rift. Or was Kelly dead too? If Kerslake had killed her why hadn't Dee reported her missing? He stopped. Impossible to imagine that Dee had also been involved. Not impossible, he reminded himself. It would not be the first time such a thing had happened.

Photographs of Kelly in her early teens showed her to be attractive. There might have been some friction between the two females if Kerslake had shown any interest in the younger one.

'Half an hour,' Barry said. 'In his office. I've got to go, Campbell wants to see me about something.'

16

And for half an hour DCI Roper did nothing but lean back in his chair, his hands behind his head, and gaze at the ceiling. There was no inspiration there. 'Dammit,' he cursed as the minutes ticked by, 'I just can't believe he did it.'

'Come in.' Superintendent Thorne's nasal Brummie accent was frequently mimicked by those under him and he knew it. It caused him no concern, far better that than being discussed in a derogatory manner as Ross had been before him. Ross, who had to go because he was bent. Thorne often reflected on the dangers of power. Ross had achieved a modicum of it and had abused it, ruining a hitherto unblemished career.

'Morning, Mike.' Ian closed the door behind him. Only in private did they address each other by their first names. There was an accepted, but different form of salutation amongst officers within every division.

'I won't keep you long. The Mercer girl hasn't been located and for all I know she's married or moved to Australia. However, I feel we should keep looking.'

'I agree,' Ian said quickly.

Thorne studied him for several seconds. 'The case is officially closed so I don't want a lot of time and manpower wasted – I just want you to bear it in mind, you understand?'

Ian did. Inquiries were to continue but in such a way that they would not interfere with any other work in progress.

'That's it then.' Thorne smiled ambiguously and was already checking his watch. 'Oh, one more thing. We sent someone to speak to Kerslake. His story remains the same.'

Ian nodded and left the room. Kerslake had said that he and Kelly got on reasonably well and he had not foreseen any problems. One evening during the school summer holiday he had returned to learn from Dee that she had moved out and was sharing a flat with a friend. He did not know where and Dee did not seem willing to discuss it. He had been surprised as her GCSE results were excellent and he had believed she intended staying on at school.

'What did he want?' Barry poked his head around the door, which was ajar. 'Seems fair enough to me,' he commented when he learned the contents of the one-sided conversation. 'If she is dead it doesn't necessarily mean Kerslake killed her.'

'Absolutely true.'

'Unless he's lying, Kelly was there one minute, gone the next. The mother might have done it.'

'You're joking.'

'It's not a particularly amusing subject.'

'My apologies. I didn't spot the mood. I thought a weekend off might have mellowed you somewhat.'

'Oh, shut up, Barry and let's decide how we're going to play this.'

An hour later they had drawn up a rough plan of action. All members of the CID would be informed that they were still looking for Kelly Mercer but it was not to take priority. If any information came to light it was to be passed to Ian, Barry or DC Brenda Gibbons.

Ian made a few notes ready for the briefing. Kelly's headmistress and year tutor had both been seen but only in the hope that they might have an idea of her whereabouts. The girls who had been her contemporaries had left school either the previous year to go on to further education or, like Kelly, three years ago as soon as they were legally able to. Kelly was not the victim therefore no time had been wasted in tracing her peers.

Once the available personnel were assembled Ian leant against the edge of a desk, his legs stretched out in front of him, and waited until they had settled down. It was a disparate group who pulled out chairs and got coffee from the machine in the corridor. He studied them. Barry was already seated as, in Ian's presence, he was conscious of his lack of height; he was, as usual, immaculately dressed but his other bugbear was the thinning, pale hair which he wore swept back over a freckled crown. Alan Campbell – ginger hair and thin moustache; pale blue eyes and skin which fried in the sun – could be nothing but Scottish. Markham; enigmatic, glowering and as fit as hell; short cropped hair; cold eyes and a smile which was terrifying. He was single, unattached and liked to work alone and most people preferred that he did. And, ah, the delectable Brenda Gibbons. Her long brown hair gleamed reddish in the sunlight as she took a seat on the window ledge. Her limbs were rounded and smooth, her face, fresh and open. She was another one who chose to keep her private life just that. Ian had only recently learned that she had been through a painful divorce.

'Everybody ready? Okay. The Mercer case . . .' Ian looked across the room as Markham made a deep-throated sound. 'You said something?'

'No, sir. I merely groaned.'

It was an honest, if typical response. Ian ignored it; to do otherwise would be a waste of breath. Fortunately Markham was a little less sour with the general public and there were few who had secured more arrests. 'Owen Kerslake's banged up awaiting trial for the murder of his common-law wife. Or should I say partner these days? As you're all aware, the daughter still hasn't come forward and the possibility of Kelly Mercer having met an untimely end must have occurred to you. The Super wants her found, but not at the expense of other cases. We're going to take it gently. I want DC Gibbons to go back to the school and speak to Kelly's teachers and, if possible, to obtain a list of her classmates during her last term there. After that we'll divide the ones still in Rickenham Green between us and then, only if necessary, go further afield. These girls will be nineteen or twenty now, young women, not schoolchildren any longer.

'Start with any particular friends, Brenda, and we'll take it from there. I don't want anyone to forget this is a limited exercise.' This was added for Ian's own benefit. He would have liked a full-scale operation.

As the officers dispersed to their desks or set off on outside business, Ian detained Markham. 'What're you working on?'

'Tying up the rape case.'

'Ah, yes. Well, if you've got any spare time it might be an idea to do a spot of door-knocking.'

'Culver Road?'

'Culver Road.'

Markham required no further instructions. Previous door-to-door inquiries had centred upon Dee Mercer, Owen Kerslake and anyone else who might have visited number 9; now they were to be focused upon the daughter.

Ian walked across the mock marble floor of the spacious

reception area where the desk sergeant was taking details from an agitated man. An elderly woman and a young blonde in a short skirt waited for attention in the plastic chairs which lined one wall. The briefing had been held in the general office where most of the detectives were housed. It was open-plan and each desk had a computer terminal and at least one telephone. At times it bore an uncanny resemblance to Ian's idea of Bedlam and he forgot how easily he had once worked under such circumstances. Upstairs were individual offices, the typing pool and a couple of rooms which held broken furniture and old files. The canteen was in the basement and it was there that Ian was heading.

Barry had beaten him to it. 'I'm not staying long, but I needed this before I go back to the joys of the Cooper family.' He had a mug of coffee into which, Ian noticed, he stirred three spoonfuls of sugar.

'Which one is it this time, Sam or Joe?'

'The sister.'

'Rachel?' Ian arched his brows. They were what might be described as a problem family, except that *they* were all happy enough, the problems belonged to those with whom they came into contact. Which parent had been responsible for the biblical names of their offspring was a mystery especially as it was doubtful either had ever set foot in a church, not even on their wedding day because no such ceremony had ever taken place. They were incompetent criminals and Ian wondered if it was because their natural milieu seemed to be interview rooms and the cells. Rachel, it appeared, was shocked and astounded that half a dozen brand new microwave ovens and an equal number of radio-cassette players had found their way into her shed without her knowledge. More surprising was that similar items had been found at her parents' home.

'Life's just full of concidences, but some are more believable than others,' Barry commented wryly.

Ian smiled. 'I know. I've always found it amazing that thieves apparently choose a complete stranger's property in which to store their stolen goods.' He finished his coffee, finding the aroma of chips and burgers and bacon unappetising.

When he was hungry it was a different matter and he had to conquer the urge to buy something to eat, but Moira had poached him a couple of eggs that morning, an unusual wifely action of late, so temptation was held safely at bay.

He felt almost happy when he left Barry to finish his own coffee. His instincts would be proved right and Superintendent Thorne, although not actually having expressed the opinion, seemed to agree with him. Why else would he authorise the continued search for Kelly Mercer?

DC Brenda Gibbons was dressed in jeans, her flowing hair in a pony tail. Mostly she favoured loose-fitting dresses which were washable and creaseproof but the washing machine had sprung a leak and she was running out of clean clothes. If she was to visit the comprehensive school she might as well call at home and fill a bin liner and dump the lot at the launderette on the way.

She was in a strange mood and suspected her restlessness was due to the onset of spring. It was warm enough to wind the window down and she did so once she had driven out of the station car-park and negotiated the lights at the junction with Saxborough Road.

Having decided that a service wash was the practical answer, she left the bag in the hands of an overalled attendant and continued her journey to the school. Her own education had taken place in a similar establishment, but one which was situated in less salubrious surroundings – although it was doubtful if her fellow puils had either noticed or cared. Having been removed from the care of an alcoholic mother and placed with foster parents, she had attended a graffiti-ridden concrete complex in south London. From that time forward she had railed against social workers who had wanted to move her again, this time from the only place where she had been happy in her short life. Fortunately their efforts failed.

Brenda bit her lip as the memories returned. It was wrong to carry out a one-woman crusade but she was still trying to prove that background did not matter, that it was who you were and what you achieved which counted. 'Everyone's got

21

a choice,' she muttered as she headed towards the main entrance, meaning a choice between getting on with life or kicking against it. The theory that the blame for the actions of thugs lay not with them was anathema to her.

She walked down the deserted corridors, her footsteps echoing. The only sounds were muted voices from rooms in which classes were being conducted. Finding the administration offices she told a secretary that Jean Adams was expecting her and was shown to the headmistress's room.

'It does surprise me,' Mrs Adams admitted when she learned that Kelly Mercer had not responded to the news and that they could not trace her. 'Mind you, we thought she'd return to school that September, she was a bright girl, she could have gone far. And now this.' She raised her hands in despair. 'It's just so unlike her. Kelly was one of the more thoughtful girls.'

'Do you know all the pupils?' There were over a thousand. Brenda wondered how she could be so sure about Kelly. She studied the headmistress whilst she spoke. Jean Adams was small and neat with a kind face although she seemed a little tired. Her hair was soft and brown, as were her eyes. She had added her own touches to her office to make it more feminine.

'Not all of them,' she admitted, 'but by the time they reach their GCSE year I'm familiar with most of them and I pay special attention to those who intend staying on. That's why I can remember Kelly. And, naturally,' she smiled, 'I have had time to read through her file since you warned me you were coming.'

It was an honest reply.

'Would there be any point in my speaking to Phillip Havers?' Havers was the deputy head and had been acting headmaster during the two terms when Jean had taken compassionate leave to care for her dying husband.

'I doubt it. His interests lie more in the smooth running of the school rather than the pupils themselves. That, and the reputation of the school,' she added rather acerbicly. 'However, if you want details of her friends you'd better speak to Pat Reynolds. She was Kelly's year tutor and she's still with us. I can arrange somewhere private for you to talk.'

22

'Thank you, I'd appreciate that. How many of the staff who would have taught Kelly in her final year are still here?'

The smile broadened. 'Ah, now that is something Phillip would be able to help you with. Excuse me one moment.' Jean Adams picked up the telephone receiver and made a brief call.

Ten minutes later, at the end of a period, a slender but mousy female joined Brenda in the room set aside for the interview. Pat Reynolds had been at Rickenham Comprehensive for ten years.

'Yes, Kelly was bright. Not brilliant, you understand, but she could have made it to university. A real university.' Her final comment gave Brenda an insight into what Pat Reynolds felt about the modern phenomenon of calling all places of higher education by that title. Brenda did not have a monopoly on strong viewpoints.

'What can you tell me about her character? Was there anything about her which made her stand out?'

There was a pause as the question was seriously considered. 'No, there was nothing unusual. Well, unless you count the fact that she was exceptionally well adjusted for a girl of that age. I think she was rather adult for her years. Perhaps it came of not having a father. I did hear that someone had moved in with her mother, but don't ask me where. These things have a habit of trickling through the grapevine. I always assumed that when Kelly didn't return to school it was either because he had refused to help support her for a further two years or because his presence had driven her away from home. Girls of sixteen are more than capable of fending for themselves these days.'

'Sixteen?'

'Yes. I went over her records with Mrs Adams. Kelly's birthday fell during the first week of the summer holidays, she would have been sixteen.'

If Pat Reynolds read the *Rickenham Herald*, as did most people in the town, she would have known that Kelly disappeared during the second week of August nearly three years previously. And only recently the paper had carried an article headed 'Missing Daughter Still Sought'.

'Who were Kelly's best friends?'

Pat Reynolds pursed her thin mouth. She had bad skin but did nothing to disguise it. 'She was a popular girl but I think she was closest to Michelle Short and Lizzie Conrad. Michelle went to Newcastle University last year but Lizzie left at the same time as Kelly. She works as a receptionist at the Duke of Clarence.'

Brenda made a note of the names. 'Boyfriends?'

'Not that I was aware of, not in school anyway, but girls of that age are more advanced than their male counterparts. There might have been someone she met outside. May I ask you something? Do you think something's happened to Kelly? You see, I find it impossible to believe she wouldn't react to news of her mother's murder, whatever her circumstances. Surely she can't not have heard about it.'

'We'd just like to find her to ask her some questions.' Brenda smiled kindly. The evasive answer would have to suffice. Before she left she ascertained that Pat Reynolds had not suspected any problems at home and that Kelly had shown no signs of unhappiness or anxiety.

'I think she would have come to me if there were problems. After all, that's partly what I'm here for.'

When Brenda returned to the car a group of first-year children were gawkily taking part in track events on one of the marked-out playing fields. She stood and watched for several minutes, able to hear the master's whistle and some of his shouted instructions. The scene looked vaguely chaotic. She grimaced. It would not be so bad today, she thought, but she used to dread freezing afternoons on the hockey field.

Pat Reynolds had taken her along the corridor to see Phillip Havers. He was a cold individual and resentful of the interruption but had provided her with a list of the names of all the staff who had been at the school in Kelly's final year. Efficiently, he had underlined those with whom she would have come into direct contact and placed an asterisk against the names of those who had left during that year, whether or not they had taught her. A second sheet of paper contained the names of her classmates. Phillip Havers was indeed a thorough administrator.

*

'That's great, Brenda. Thanks. Care to join us at the Feathers later?'

She hesitated then said she would although she did not feel like it. For far too long she had intended rebuilding her social life but the impetus was missing. Drinking with the boys was not really the solution but it was, she supposed, better than nothing. And she must remember to collect her washing before the launderette closed at ten.

DCI Roper studied the lists Brenda had had the foresight to copy. Michelle Short, now at Newcastle, would be easy enough to contact if the need arose. Lizzie Conrad would be easier still. He picked up the external telephone and asked the switchboard to put him through to the Duke of Clarence Hotel. 'Sod's law,' he said when he learned that she was not on duty until the following afternoon. Bearing in mind Thorne's instructions he decided to wait. Calling around at her home address could not be described as taking a casual approach. 'And I don't like it.'

'What?' Barry continued running his eye down the lists in case any of the names meant anything to him.

'People forcing their Christian names on me when I've never even met them. Why not just give the name of the hotel?'

'They're trained to do it. Besides . . . no, it doesn't matter.' He could not be bothered to point out that the Chief was a stickler for insisting upon knowing exactly to whom he was speaking when he used the telephone. Surely it saved time if they gave him a name first? There were a lot of things the Chief claimed to dislike and Barry was not about to slap the rump of one of his favourite hobby horses when it seemed to be galloping strongly without any assistance from him. 'Do you think this means anything?' He indicated the asterisked name of a member of staff. 'Derek Cavanagh. He left at the same time as the Mercer girl.'

Ian glanced at his own copy. The same thought had crossed his mind. There seemed to have been plenty of movement amongst the teachers, unlike in his own day when the masters at his all-boy establishment tended to remain there until they retired. Could it be that simple, that Kelly Mercer and Cavanagh had done a bunk?

25

Between September and the following July one female member of staff had retired and had been replaced by another who was still at Rickenham Comprehensive; a second had left at the end of the spring term to have a baby but she did not seem relevant as she had never taught Kelly. Someone called Jack Farraday had come and gone during the course of one term but Phillip Havers had made it clear his position was temporary, he was a supply teacher filling in until a full-time replacement could join them. Maggie Simpson, too, had ended her contract just before the Easter break.

Derek Cavanagh; with the word 'History' typed next to his name. He was definitely worth talking to as he had taught Kelly. 'Get on to the head, Barry, and see if you can find out why Cavanagh left. It doesn't say here. There's a directory of teachers, or some such thing – if he's still trying to drum knowledge into the little buggers' heads he'll be in it. Ask them to look him up if they don't know.'

'I thought the Super said – '

'I know what he said, but one telephone call can hardly be described as calling out the troops, now, can it? Get on with it and I'll let you buy me a pint later.'

4

A serious assault charge took up most of the following day and it was not until late afternoon that Ian was able to spare the time to visit the Duke of Clarence to speak to Lizzie Conrad. If she had been a confidante of Kelly's she might know if there had been more than a teacher/pupil relationship between Kelly and Derek Cavanagh, who had, Barry had discovered, left the school for unspecified personal reasons. If it was simply a case of her having run away with a married teacher, all well and good. It might be immoral but it was not illegal. Cavanagh was now at a school in Northamptonshire – on the same salary level, so promotion had not been his reason for leaving.

Ian drove into the car-park behind the Duke of Clarence. Most of the vehicles were top-of-the-range models. It was a large, ivy-covered building and catered for people who put comfort and service above modernity and entertainment. There was no swimming pool, no sauna and gym, no disco attached to the premises. There was also nothing noisier in the bar than the chink of glasses and subdued conversation between guests who were enjoying an early evening drink. Ian would have liked to be doing so himself but that would have to wait.

He crossed the thickly carpeted foyer and approached the wooden reception counter behind which two girls were busy booking people in. Along the walls were squashy sofas interspersed with potted ferns which gave the place a vaguely Edwardian air. Quiet money stayed at the Duke; it would not suit the *nouveaux riches* or lottery winners.

'Can I help you, sir?' One of the two brunettes was appraising him with a questioning smile. Perhaps his slightly creased grey trousers and his tweed jacket seemed out of place to her, but Ian had known a stinking rich couple who both looked down at heel and who, to his amazement, preferred to eat in their kitchen where a milk bottle could be seen on the table. Real money, he supposed, freed you from the restraining conventions of the middle classes.

Ian returned the smile. She was an attractive girl. 'Indeed you can.' He showed her his identification. 'I'd like a few words with your colleague – and I wonder if you could organise somewhere suitable for us to talk?' Her name badge told him she was called Geraldine Seraphin and he was pleased to note both names had been etched upon it even if she did answer the telephone using only her first.

Geraldine went out through a door behind her and returned in a very short time. Coming around to the foyer she said, 'If you'd like to follow me, Lizzie will be with you in a minute.'

The room into which he was shown was some sort of office where, hidden from the guests, there were several computer terminals. Ian sat in one of the chairs and waited.

Lizzie Conrad opened the door and gave him a smile so

dazzling his stomach churned. Her auburn hair was tied back showing a high forehead and green eyes. 'I've arranged for some coffee,' she told him. 'It won't be long.'

Her straightforward manner and lack of anxiety showed she had nothing to fear from the police and it seemed that the policy of the hotel was to extend hospitality to anyone who came through its portals. 'I'd like to ask you a few questions about Kelly Mercer.'

'Kelly?' She seemed genuinely puzzled. 'I haven't seen her for a couple of years. Nearly three, in fact. It was terrible, what happened to her mother.'

'Did you know Dee Mercer?'

Lizzie shook her head and Ian smelled her perfume. 'I saw her once or twice but Kelly didn't seem keen on taking people home. She used to come to my house or else we'd go out.'

It was an interesting statement. 'Was there any reason for that?'

'I – oh, just a minute.' She got up to take a silver tray containing a matching coffee set and cups and saucers from the porter who had brought it. On a plate were some biscuits which Ian decided to ignore, wondering why matters of self-control were always so much easier in the presence of an attractive woman. 'What was I saying? Oh, yes. I don't know, but I don't think she took anyone home. I didn't think about it at the time.'

'Were you Kelly's best friend?'

'No. We were good friends, but I think she was closer to Michelle. Michelle Short,' she added. 'She's at university now.'

'Ah.' Ian had not prepared any questions and as Lizzie seemed intelligent it seemed better to let her talk.

'Is she in some sort of trouble?' The green eyes widened.

'What makes you think that?'

Lizzie shrugged. 'Nothing in particular. It's just that if you need to know things, wouldn't it be easier to speak to Kelly herself?'

'Yes. If we knew where she was.'

'Hasn't she come back?'

'Back from where?' Ian watched carefully for the reaction.

'I don't know. It was all very odd. We left school at the end of that term, I knew I wasn't going back as I'd already got a job here, but I thought Kelly was going to take her A levels. I saw her twice after that, then, when I got my first week's wages, I rang up to ask if she wanted to come out and celebrate. Her mother said she'd left home, that she'd found a flat and a job. I couldn't believe it, she hadn't said a word to me. And I haven't heard from her since.'

And nor has anyone else, Ian thought, realising the implications.

'It just wasn't like Kelly,' Lizzie continued, obviously glad to be able to express what she had felt at the time. 'She was usually so thoughtful.'

Pat Reynolds, her year tutor, had described the girl as well adjusted and mature; she was also, apparently, thoughtful. Not many sixteen-year-olds were such paragons of virtue. 'What do you know about Owen Kerslake?'

Lizzie frowned and reached up to tighten the band holding back her hair. Ian averted his eyes. Through the polyester-cotton of her uniform blouse he saw the lacy outline of her bra as the material stretched across her breasts. 'The man who moved in with her mother, you mean? She liked him. She said she thought he was all right.' Ian was treated to another of the smiles. 'When you're sixteen and trying to be cool "all right" is high praise.'

He grinned back. Lizzie was only nineteen now. And when Ian was sixteen he had given no thought to the impression he was making on others; his only interests were football and the Sea Scouts which he had joined to get away from his elderly parents. Lizzie was mocking herself at an earlier age as if she had seen it all. Maybe, he thought, she has.

'Thinking about it, I wonder if Kelly had always wanted to leave school but felt she couldn't, not if it meant her mother would be alone. Perhaps having Owen there gave her the chance to escape.'

'Escape?'

'I don't mean that anything was wrong, it was just that Kelly, being the sort of girl she is, would have felt it her duty to stay.'

Ian asked about boyfriends but Lizzie knew of none, other than in the sense of friendship only. 'Derek Cavanagh, he taught you both history in your last year, didn't he? How did you find him?'

'He was a good teacher, he got people interested and not many failed the exam. Oh.' She blushed, suddenly realising what he was after. 'If you mean did I fancy him, well, yes, a bit. We all did, he was very good-looking.'

'Including Kelly?'

'Maybe, she never said. Anyway, it was a bit of fun. He had a wife and two small daughters.'

If Kelly did not discuss her harmless fantasies as the other girls did, it seemed more, not less, likely that something had been going on, and having a wife and children was no guarantee of fidelity. 'I had to ask. They both left at the same time.'

Lizzie's laugh showed what a ridiculous theory she thought it to be. 'I can't imagine Kelly being so stupid. She had her whole life in front of her, she wanted to live, to do all sorts of things. That's why I thought she would go back to school, so's she could get to university.'

There was nothing more Lizzie could tell him and he had to leave. 'Thank you for your help. I hope it won't cause any problems with the management.'

'No, Mr Sherwood said I could be as long as was necessary.'

Back in the car Ian sat for several moments watching a line of trees which acted as a windbreak to the lawn beyond them swaying gently. Kelly was popular; Kelly had no domestic problems; Kelly liked her surrogate stepfather; Kelly was doing well at school and had hoped to get to university; Kelly had not fallen out with a boyfriend. All these facts made the enigma of her sudden disappearance harder to swallow. He started the engine, backed out of his parking space and turned into the main road. The evening was chilly but he recalled other years when, just as the days began to lengthen and the clocks went forward, winter made a temporary come-back as if nature was warning humanity not to take things for granted.

Ian drove straight home, a concession which he knew would

please Moira, but it was a wasted gesture. On the kitchen table of 14 Belmont Terrace was a scribbled note saying she had gone to the library and would be home about seven thirty. He settled for a cup of coffee and switched on the television.

DC Brenda Gibbons had, in quiet moments, begun going through the list of Kelly Mercer's classmates. It was a simple task as the addresses where they lived when they had attended Rickenham Comprehensive were typed neatly below their names, along with any telephone numbers. Alphabetically, she rang those whose parents were subscribers. Many of the youths had left home and, without causing alarm or anger, she managed to elicit their present whereabouts from their families, reassuring them that their offspring were not in any trouble. Those who had left the area altogether she ruled out. They could be contacted later if the Chief thought it necessary. Some had jobs in the town, others had gone away to college and one or two were married.

Working her way down the list she chewed the end of her biro when she came to the name Ann Proctor. The name itself meant nothing but the address was Culver Road. The Mercers had lived in Culver Road. If the two girls had not only been in the same class but were also neighbours, Ann Proctor was definitely worth speaking to.

'Problems?'

Brenda looked up. DS Markham was standing beside her, his expression, as usual, unreadable. It was only when he smiled, or produced what, for Markham, passed as a smile, that anyone was aware he had emotions. The paradox was that Markham's smile did not signify happiness, it was more of a threat. 'No, not problems, just thinking. Where's the Chief?'

'Taking a statement from another girl who's come forward claiming to be a victim of attempted rape. Judy Robbins is with him,' Markham continued, seeing Brenda's raised eyebrows. 'Should be nearly finished now.'

Brenda put her copies of the lists into a folder and locked it in her drawer. Having telephoned the Proctor household she

31

had discovered that Ann still lived at home. Had it not been eleven o'clock in the morning she would have acted upon her own initiative and gone to see the girl but right now she would be seated beside the check-out counter in Fine Fare, unless she was taking her tea break. However, she was certain that, once the Chief knew of the double relationship, someone would be sent over to Culver Road. Meanwhile she went upstairs to study a copy of the Kerslake file. If the Proctors lived only four doors away they would have been questioned by the B team who were on door-to-door, if not interviewed at length afterwards.

Ian sighed. The man who had been charged with the rape of a twenty-three-year-old woman had admitted to one other incident of indecent assault. Since his arrest two more females had come forward. The first had sounded genuine but the woman he had just spent an hour with had altered her story several times. PC Judy Robbins was in agreement with him; she, too, thought the woman was lying. 'She tripped up over almost everything,' Judy commented when they had left the interview room. 'She might just be an attention seeker.'

'I got the same impression, but you know what it's like these days, we have to be so careful.' It was a real problem. Unless there was physical violence involved it was one person's word against another's and even if a woman led a man on almost to the point of no return, it was still rape if she said no at the last minute and he did not comply with her wishes.

'Anything new on Kerslake?'

Ian shook his head and smiled. He was fond of Judy Robbins. She was conscientious and hard-working – although she would never be more than a PC – but it was more than that, she was a friend. She had looked after Mark when he was little and was one of those people who could cheer you up just by their presence. Now into her thirties, she was still unmarried and had put on weight since the days when she was new to Rickenham. Perhaps because he was married to Moira Ian had fought against middle age. Judy seemed to be settling into it far too young.

'Do you still think he's innocent?'

'That's no longer for me to say.'

'That means you do.' She grinned and Ian had to laugh.

'It's illogical, I know, especially as there was no robbery and no sexual assault and everything points in his direction, but . . .' He shrugged.

'But you've got a gut feeling. I know, I've seen you like this before.'

'It's never gone this far, though. We've nearly always got the right bloke before we make an arrest. Kerslake won't stand a chance in court and if the Chief Constable thought there was enough evidence, our hands are tied.' Ian spotted DC Gibbons hovering near his office. 'I'll see you later, Judy.'

Brenda told him what she had discovered and was instructed to speak to Ann Proctor at the first opportunity.

'She started work at eight, sir. Her mother said she'll be home around five.'

Brenda went back to the general office where she had other things to attend to but her concentration was not as good as it usually was. The Kerslake file showed that the Proctors and their daughter had made statements. Sean Proctor had been at work all day, in Ipswich, and therefore it was impossible for him to have been around at lunchtime. His wife had walked into the town centre at nine to do her weekly shopping, a taxi dropped her home around eleven. It was her day off because she, too, was employed by Fine Fare and she had worked the previous Saturday. After she had unpacked the groceries she had cleaned the three-bedroomed house from top to bottom and done several machine-loads of washing. It was her usual routine for a day off and therefore easily remembered. She had not left the house again that day. There was nothing unusual about the senior Proctors' statements but Ann's, although reasonable as far as it went, was interesting for its omissions. She had not mentioned that she had been at school with Kelly and her words seemed to imply that she hardly knew the Mercers.

Needing to be sure of her facts before she went back to Culver Road, Brenda reread the whole file.

Owen Kerslake was forty years old, the same age as Dee. He had moved to Rickenham Green in 1990, soon after the break-up of his marriage. He met Dee at the fish and chip shop where she had worked for the eight years prior to her death but he had not moved in with her until three years later although they had been seeing one another on a regular basis.

Brenda wondered if this was because, both of them having been in bad relationships before, they were extra cautious about committing themselves or whether, because of Kerslake's past history, Dee was taking no chances. Kerslake had been picked up six years previously for having sexual intercourse with a girl of thirteen, one who could have passed for several years older, as many could. The girl's mother had found some sexually explicit photographs of her in her bedroom. She had blamed Kerslake who had, at the time, been in the process of decorating their house. On one occasion only, they had been left alone together. The charges had been dropped but the damage was done. Kerslake's wife was a great believer in the adage of there being no smoke without fire. She had thrown him out.

There was a note in the file, in the Chief's handwriting. He had spoken to the officer who had made the arrest and learned that it was more than probable that the young girl's boyfriend, about whom the parents knew nothing, was responsible and that she had accused Kerslake to protect him. All hearsay, of course, and it might be that she had been telling the truth. However, it did seem unlikely that Kerslake could have taken advantage of the unexpected opportunity and also photographed the girl in such a short space of time. Nevertheless, maybe erring on the side of safety, Dee had decided not to put the relationship on a more permanent standing until Kelly was past the dangerous age.

After Dee's murder the house had been thoroughly searched. There was no Polaroid camera, in fact, no camera of any description, but that, again, proved nothing one way or the other. It seemed to Brenda to be a non-fact typical of the case.

What surprised her was that it was Kerslake who had volunteered this information about himself; they might never have known about it otherwise, as no formal charges were made. He also admitted he had told Dee, wanting everything to be out in the open from the start.

But if he was guilty of the first offence had he been tempted by Kelly? It might be the reason she left, without telling her mother why, so as not to hurt her. Or, as had been mooted, had he abused the girl then killed her to protect himself?

Brenda tried to put it out of her mind and applied herself to her computer terminal where she was attempting to make sense of a spate of house burglaries which appeared random but where the thieves were targeting certain goods and leaving other, more valuable items behind.

'Fancy some lunch?' DS Barry Swan poked his head around the door of Ian's office. He was pale and there was a worried crease bisecting his forehead.

Ian stretched and stood up, reaching for his jacket which was over the back of his chair. 'Why not?'

Together they went downstairs, crossed the reception area, pushed through the revolving doors and walked down the short path between the raised flowerbeds on to the street. The sky was a clear blue but the wind was from the east. Ian buttoned his jacket and shoved his hands in his pockets. Barry's raincoat flapped around his calves and his hair was blown sideways.

They paused on the wide pavement as shoppers and office workers on their way to buy sandwiches walked by on either side of them.

'Where to?'

'I'm easy,' Ian replied.

They continued walking towards the town centre and the High Street. They passed a row of boutique-type shops which were followed by several fast food outlets. They were beyond the Indian restaurant they favoured and the tea-rooms which served proper Welsh rarebit where they sometimes ate. Barry liked the Three Feathers, known to most people simply as the Feathers. They served the brand of lager he preferred as well as a fair selection of meals. Feeling generous and because he could see that Ian was in danger of succumbing to one of his fits of mild depression, he suggested the Crown which bordered the Green.

Ian glanced at Barry in surprise. 'Fair enough,' he said and followed him down the alley between a row of cottages which was a short cut.

There were only a couple of spare tables because they had left it late but most of the customers had finished eating and would soon be leaving. They went to the bar.

Bob Jones was in typical pose, leaning on the Guinness dispenser and listening to the latest gossip from a couple of regulars. 'Never,' they heard him say, 'not in a million years.' Without seeming to have noticed their arrival he reached beneath the counter for a glass and placed it under the Adnam's hand pump, then took a second glass and filled it with lager. These he placed in front of Ian and Barry, nodding his head in agreement with something one of the locals was telling him. As he reached out a hand for the money he finally looked up and grinned. 'How are you, my lovelies?' he inquired in his lilting Welsh voice. He handed Barry the change and rested his hands on his ample stomach as he watched Ian take his first satisfied sip.

'Up to standard.' Ian placed the glass on the bar.

'What's new then?' Bob leaned forward in anticipation.

'Not a lot.'

Bob moved away to serve another customer. He had known Ian a long time. 'Not a lot' meant plenty but he was not about to be privy to it.

'Can we order some grub?' Ian said when he had finished serving. Bob got the pad and a pen from the back shelf and made a note of what they wanted. 'We'll be over there.' Ian indicated the seat in the window which had just been vacated.

'Why? That's the question I keep asking myself. Why would Kerslake want to kill her?'

'Usual reasons. Jealousy, a temper he couldn't control, perhaps she nagged.'

36

'Come off it, you know as much as I do. From all accounts they got on well enough.'

'And you know that what goes on behind closed doors is often a lot different from what the public see.'

'I don't think it applies in this case. For a start, that chip shop bloke's known Dee for eight years. He said she was always cheerful but even more so after Kerslake moved in and she's never shown up with any bruising. The neighbours bear this out as well. He had nothing to gain, it wasn't even as if the house was hers.'

Barry had been responsible for checking Kerslake's position as far as the council property went. From their investigations they knew Dee's savings were meagre, and they had not been able to come up with any evidence that either Dee or Owen had been involved with a third party. Even if they had been, murder would have been a drastic step to take as they were not married. 'The more I think about it, the more inclined I am to agree with you. For instance, if he was a violent man, or a row had erupted that day, it's unlikely she'd have kept her back to him. You don't, do you, when you're arguing? It's natural to face one another. What beats me is that there's no other candidate.'

Ian remained silent. He was certain there had to be and, although he had to tread carefully for fear of bringing the Chief Constable's wrath on his head, he would continue gently probing until he was satisfied one way or the other.

'It's possible,' Barry continued, talking just for the sake of it, 'that he had some kind of brain-storm.'

'Oh, yes, that explains it all. He drives home for no apparent reason – he's got his flask and sandwiches and newspaper and he keeps all his gear in the van, don't forget – sees his wife cutting up steak for a stew or whatever and decides to do the same to her. Sanity returns rapidly because he then scrubs the knife under the kitchen tap, makes sure there's no blood on himself and returns to the park to eat his cheese and pickle in granary.'

Barry felt his face flush, something he was unable to control and which he hated. 'It was only a suggestion, there's no need to get . . . here's the food.'

37

Connie Jones, equally flushed, but from the heat in the kitchen, sailed across the bar with a loaded tray. 'Ian. Barry. How are you?'

'We're fine, thanks.'

'Good,' she said, seeing that that was far from true. She placed a chicken salad sandwich in front of Barry and a portion of beef Madras and rice to the side of Ian's glass.

'Don't you get enough of that?' Barry brandished the knife which he was about to dip into the mayonnaise in the direction of the curry.

'No. Besides, home-made tastes entirely different whatever you do to it. I can never decide which I prefer.'

They ate in silence, stopping only once for Ian to replenish their glasses with a half-pint each. 'I think Brenda might be on to something.' Ian wiped his mouth with a paper serviette which he then screwed up to disguise the yellowish stain.

'In what way?'

Ian explained what she had deduced from Ann Proctor's initial statement. 'Seems odd not to mention she'd been to school with the daughter.'

'It was three years ago.'

'Yes. But even so . . . Anyway, it might be an idea to speak to the residents of Culver Road again. Find out what else they're not saying. Brenda's willing to put in a bit of her own time, so am I.'

'This sounds suspiciously as if you're asking for volunteers.'

'Thanks, Barry, that's very decent of you.'

'You bastard,' he muttered as he shrugged his arms into his raincoat.

Markham, too, had said he didn't mind a bit of door-knocking on his way home. The Chief had warned them all they were to tread very softly. The case was officially closed, they dared not risk any complaints and they were to take it in turns, not turn up in force, which would cause unnecessary gossip and draw attention to themselves. He had done some night surveillance work recently and was due a few hours off. He left the headquarters building at three thirty and clocked off.

He went on foot, as he did at every opportunity. Walking briskly he did not notice the chill wind. There were only a few cars parked in Culver Road as those at work had not yet returned. He knew to avoid number 17, four doors away from the Mercer house which now stood empty, because Brenda would be there later. There was no response from the first house he called at. He did not knock a second time but made a mental note to ask someone else to call there. He had started at the opposite end of the road where the high numbers were, working on the basis that those who knew least about the Mercers and Kerslake might be more inclined to gossip about them.

At the next house a young woman stood before him. A toddler was in her arms and in the background he heard a very small baby wailing. From her stance and the bulge of her stomach it seemed as if there might be another one on the way, unless she had not got her figure back yet. He was reminded of Barry's loss and thought how unfair life was. Here was a young female, worn out well before her time, whose expression hinted at a resentful dissatisfaction with her lot, whilst Lucy was heartbroken to have lost her baby. Lucy, though, was nearly thirty, this girl was no more than twenty-one or two.

'Is it about the murder?' She looked at him with dull, lifeless eyes. 'If so, you'd better come in.'

Markham followed her into the living-room. It was sparsely furnished but surprisingly clean and tidy. 'Mrs Prout, isn't it?'

She nodded but did not ask him to sit down, neither did she do so herself.

'I know you've already been asked some questions, but this time we're interested in Dee's daughter, Kelly. Did you know her?'

'Yes. We've been here just over four years now. We're on the waiting list for a bigger house. When the next one's born it can share to start with, I've got one of each, see, but when it's older we'll need more space. She babysat a couple of times.'

Markham thought she had lost track of the question. But he had been right about the baby although he doubted if the Prouts would be given a four-bedroomed house in a hurry.

'So you knew her quite well?'

'Not really. Oh, do you want to sit down?'

'Thanks.' He was about to lower himself on to the settee when he noticed a soggy rusk on the side of the cushion. He moved slightly left and sat in the opposite corner. Mrs Prout remained standing and swung the child to her other hip. 'What can you tell me about her?'

'She's a nice enough girl, and she's got more patience than me, Andrew's crying never seemed to bother her. There was only the one then, of course. I never really spoke to her much, other people in the street said she was a good girl, and reliable and that she'd babysat for them, so I thought it was all right. She hasn't gone and done something, has she?'

'No, nothing like that.' Markham was studying the child. It looked far too small to be three, or nearly three. 'Were you surprised when she left home?'

'Not really. We didn't talk about what she wanted to do or anything. She certainly seemed happy enough, you know, always smiling, and really pretty, she was.' Mrs Prout bowed her head as if afraid Markham might be making comparisons. She, too, had been pretty once.

'So there were no problems you were aware of?'

'No. I used to see her and Dee go off shopping together on Saturdays, or in the school holidays. It made me wish I'd got on with my mum when I was at home. They were more like friends really. Oh, no.' Andrew, in imitation of his sister, began to cry. 'I wish she was here now to take him off my hands for an hour.' She put the child on the floor and gradually the sobs subsided.

'And Ann Proctor?'

'Ann? What's she got to do with any of this?'

'She and Kelly were classmates and, living so close, I thought they might have been friends.'

'Sorry, I can't help you. Like I said, I never really spoke to Kelly.'

Mrs Prout showed Markham to the door to the accompaniment of the unseen baby's wails. Maybe he had learned nothing but here was yet another testimonial to Kelly Mercer's good nature. Cynic that he was, Markham doubted anyone could be that saintly.

40

He decided to try a couple more houses then go home because he was in need of an early night. Next door to Mrs Prout lived an elderly couple. In the few inches afforded him by the retaining chain he saw their wrinkled faces peering at him. He was asked to hand his identification over. They scrutinised it and seemed satisfied because the door was shut then opened fully. Markham noticed that the downstairs curtains were almost closed although it was still daylight.

The couple claimed they did not know any of their neighbours and had not met Dee or Kelly. 'We keep to ourselves,' the husband told him, 'and we only allow the home help in.' They seemed to live in self-enforced imprisonment and the old man's tone implied that people who got themselves murdered probably deserved no less.

One more, he thought, then he'd radio in and let the Chief know who he had spoken to.

Pearl Rickford was more than happy to while away some time chatting. She led him down the hall to the kitchen and put the kettle on. Through the window he saw washing flapping on a rotary line. The place was spotless and smelled of Dettol. Pearl Rickford volunteered the information that she lived alone and it seemed likely that she used housework as a way to relieve her boredom.

'Kelly?' she asked, drawing pencilled eyebrows closer together as she handed him a cup of tea. 'I've known her since she was this high.' With the flat of her hand she indicated a spot about three feet above the polished flooring. 'Such a dear little thing, she was, an angel. And unlike most of them, she didn't change as she got older, she was still as sweet as ever. I used to look after her sometimes when Dee was on shifts at the hospital. That was before she started at the chip shop,' she added for clarification. 'Never knew who her father was. Dee kept that one to herself all right.'

Markham sipped his tea. It was hot and strong and had been made in a pot with leaves rather than tea-bags. Kelly's father. Had anyone investigated that angle? He did not think so.

'Still,' Pearl continued, 'none of us are blameless, are we? These things happen. I miss Kelly.' She pulled out the chair opposite Markham's and sat down. With her elbows on the

41

table she clasped her cup in both hands. 'I couldn't understand it when she went away. I was hurt she didn't come and say goodbye. She wasn't the type to have got herself in any trouble and she got on well with Owen. God, I can't believe it, he idolised Dee, you know.'

Markham bent his own elbow to take a surreptitious look at his watch. Pearl Rickman seemed prepared for a long session but the night's sleep he had missed was beginning to catch up. 'So you can't think of any reason why she suddenly took it into her head to leave?'

She frowned and shook her head. 'Wait, there was one occasion – well, it probably doesn't mean anything. She used to talk to me like a friend and one time I just got the impression there was something she wanted to tell me. She didn't though, and about a week later she'd gone.'

'Thank you, you've been a great help.' Markham stood prior to leaving.

'Have I? Come back again if you need to know anything more. You'll always be welcome.'

He nodded, thanked her for the tea and wondered why a woman of no more than forty-five should choose such a solitary existence. 'Oh, one more thing. I don't suppose you've heard from Kelly since?' If they had been close it was not impossible.

'No. I asked Dee where she'd gone but she was very evasive and I just said to send her my love. If you find her will you pass that on for me?'

'Of course.'

Out of sight of Culver Road he contacted the station to inform the duty officer whom he had seen then he continued on through the estate and emerged into the High Street through the churchyard of St Luke's. Tempted as he was to go into the Feathers he bypassed it and went home.

Brenda put on her short jacket over one of the dresses she had ironed the previous evening. The woman at the launderette had dried her things too thoroughly and the task had taken longer than she had anticipated. Swinging her car keys she

42

went out into the evening air which was less chilly than on the previous day.

She drove through Rickenham Green and turned into the council estate, parking immediately outside the Proctors' house in Culver Road. She had been on hand when Markham radioed in. Kelly Mercer, it seemed, was not only thoughtful, mature, intelligent and pretty, she had now been described as an angel. 'I think not,' she said aloud before getting out of the car. She had yet to meet a sixteen-year-old to whom that so-briquet could apply.

Several children stopped throwing a ball and stared at her with undisguised curiosity. She was a glamorous figure with her auburn-brown hair flowing around her shoulders. Once they saw she was heading towards the Proctors' house and not one of their own they continued their game, their shouts hollow in the quiet street. An electric lawnmower started up and buzzed irritatingly behind one of the houses where the grass was receiving its first cut of the year. Within seconds Brenda could smell its clean fragrance. In the house adjacent to the Proctors' a side window was open. Someone was frying liver and onions. She found it difficult to reconcile such normality with what she had witnessed at number 9.

'Get that, will you, love?' Brenda heard the shouted words clearly after she rang the bell. One short burst on an old-fashioned brass button.

The young woman who answered the door was of medium height and with a figure which would turn many heads. Her hair, a similar colour to Brenda's although more red than chestnut, swung forwards framing her face. Her high cheekbones and wide, perfectly delineated mouth made her beautiful rather than pretty. Brenda thought there must be something in the air in Culver Road for two such stunners to have been produced. Photographs of Kelly showed her to be equally attractive.

'Yes?'

'Hello, I'm Brenda Gibbons from the Rickenham Green police. Did your mother tell you I was coming?' She smiled because the girl seemed nervous.

43

'Yes. You'd better come in.'

Eileen Proctor appeared in the hall, wiping her hands on a tea towel. She glanced from her daughter to Brenda. 'Do you want to talk in private?'

'I'd prefer it.' Ann was not a minor, there was no need for a parent or guardian to be present.

'Show the lady into the front room, love. Shall I be making some tea?'

'No thanks. I won't be very long.'

Brenda grimaced when she entered the front room. It had been what she could only describe as 'preserved'. Everything looked new and she suspected the Proctors lived in the kitchen. The colour scheme was garish, there were Venetian blinds over the windows, no doubt to prevent the sun from fading the soft furnishings, but worse was the clear plastic covering which remained on the settee and two armchairs.

'What do you want to know?'

Brenda could not ascertain if Ann was naturally sullen or if she was scared. 'About Kelly. Were you a special friend of hers?'

'No.'

'I see. But you were in the same class?'

'That doesn't mean anything. So were thirty others.'

It was a good point. 'Didn't you ever play with her, when you were children?'

'Sometimes.'

'What about when she left home, did you know about that?'

'No. I told you, we weren't that close. We just chatted sometimes if we happened to see each other.'

'All right. What about Derek Cavanagh, your history teacher?'

Ann was nonplussed. She could not understand the purpose of the questions. 'I don't know what you mean.'

'Do you think Kelly liked him? Is it possible she more than liked him?'

'No. Kelly Mercer was too good for any man.' Her tone was scornful.

'Thank you, Ann. I'm sorry to have interrupted your evening.'

44

As she was shown to the front door it opened before they reached it. A muscular man in his forties entered and stared at Brenda before slowly looking her up and down. He would have been handsome if it was not for the leer. Although he wore a suit his clothes were on the flashy side, in contrast to his wife and daughter who were plainly dressed. Perhaps the choice of furnishings had been his.

'Excuse me,' Brenda said and squeezed past him, not wanting to make contact. She had felt undressed under his gaze.

In the car she scribbled a few notes. One thing was certain, Ann Proctor was lying.

Because there was nothing to go home to she returned to the station. The Chief's car was still there; she might as well report to him immediately.

'I wonder . . .' Ian said, tipping his chair back and balancing his bulk on the back legs. 'Kelly, Ann and Lizzie are all lookers.'

'And Kerslake was under suspicion for having sexual intercourse with a minor.'

'I wasn't thinking of that.'

'Oh?'

Ian shook his head. 'I don't really know what I was thinking about.'

Brenda grinned, her teeth so straight and white Ian thought it unfair. 'Too much of a coincidence, is that what you're thinking?'

'You're a witch, DC Gibbons. Now go on home and leave me to think.'

Brenda did so, then, on the spur of the moment, because she knew it was now or never, she turned left into the drive of the tennis club and asked how she could go about joining. She was given some forms and told she would have to 'play in'. It had been three years since she picked up a racket but her game had been quite good then. She would ask someone at the station to join her on the public courts before she returned the form.

With a feeling of smug satisfaction she decided she would also cook herself a proper meal. When you were alone it was too easy to exist on canteen food and sandwiches although it didn't seem to do her figure any harm.

The funeral finally took place. It was attended by the residents of Culver Road, Dee's ex-employer and two members of the CID.

There was no sign of Kelly Mercer.

Enid Mercer, Dee's mother and Kelly's grandmother, was slowly improving but was not well enough to attend the church. Wheelchair-bound, she had been knocked sideways by the news of Dee's death. So far no one had been able to question her in any depth. But that time was approaching.

5

Barry Swan was spending most evenings preparing for his inspector's exams although he was rapidly losing confidence in his ability to pass them. He was also aware that if he did so it might mean a move. He had worked for so long with Ian that he was not sure if he wanted a change. He could just forget the whole thing but, having got so far, that seemed a waste.

Lucy was sitting at the large round dining-table in the back window which overlooked a body-shop and a meat products depot. She watched an articulated lorry making the awkward manoeuvre into the yard. 'Barry . . .' she said, without turning around.

'Um?'

'I'm pregnant again.'

There was complete silence. Lucy had gone to such trouble when she told him about the first baby; she had bathed and washed her hair and worn new clothes and there had been a special, three course meal. It had all been for nothing. She had tripped and fallen down the stairs of the flats and lost the baby. Superstition dictated that she do it differently this time.

Barry was still in the armchair. He stared at her open-mouthed. It should have been a moment of joy but all he felt was fear. His mouth was dry as he said, 'That's wonderful.' Putting down his books he walked over to her and gently put his arms around her before kissing the top of her head. 'It'll be all right this time, you'll see.'

'I hope so,' she said, before bursting into tears. She had not told him immediately but waited until she was into her second month. If she got through the next four weeks she would begin to feel more confident.

Barry had been about to suggest she gave up work if she wanted. It would also spur him on with his study because they would need the extra money but it would not be doing Lucy any favours. He must let her continue as normal.

When she had stopped crying he smiled. 'That's more like it. Now, why don't we go out to eat?' He knew what was ahead of them both. Already he was being careful with words. He had not said to celebrate.

'Yes, I'd like that. I'll get a coat.'

She finally smiled properly when he held her elbow to guide her down the stairs down which she had fallen. It would be nice to be spoiled for a while.

Owen Kerslake's solicitor had arranged for one of the best defence barristers he could come up with. Owen's savings from his decorating business precluded his being awarded legal aid, but as he felt that life was not worth anything without Dee it seemed not to matter if all his money was used up. He did not want to spend half of the rest of his life in prison but he could not envisage what he would do with himself if he was released.

The solicitor, Victor Rowland, visited him several times. 'It was as I told them at the time. I went to work, I went to the park for my lunch, then I went home. I didn't do it.'

Rowland had been over and over it. Studying Kerslake's face and listening to how he responded to the questions, he, too, became convinced his client was innocent. That was when he had decided to go for the best. His job was to get him off, not to prove someone else guilty, but it worried him that Kerslake was in the dark about whether anyone

47

else could have had a motive or might have wished to harm Dee. Knowing how the police worked he was pretty certain they had not given up on their efforts at finding the daughter. Here, too, Kerslake was at a loss. He had also admitted to his previous arrest. 'Will that come out in court?' he had asked.

'No. Although it might afterwards.' If you're found guilty, he added silently, and perhaps if you're not. Someone from the press would find out. 'All right, let's go through it one more time.' He did not expect the story to change but repetition produced boredom and it could be that Kerslake might recall some minor factor which might make all the difference.

Superintendent Thorne scratched his balding pate and sniffed. Ian knew this meant he was considering the matter. 'One visit,' he finally said. 'And I mean one.'

'Thanks, Mike.' He had explained that DC Gibbons thought the Proctor girl was lying and, once more, vehemently expressed his own views of the case.

'Oh, and while you're at it, you might as well get someone from Tyneside to speak to Michelle Short.'

Ian's grin widened into a beam. Whatever Thorne was saying, it was not what he was thinking. Ian was convinced he was having second thoughts. He whistled tunelessly as he went back down the corridor to his own office.

Barry Swan had traced Cavanagh to Northamptonshire and, having spoken to someone at the school, learned that he had joined them in September 1993. He had moved to the area almost immediately after leaving Rickenham Green. Ian wondered whether he had simply been lucky, selling his own house and buying another so quickly, or whether he had arranged it in advance. He would soon find out. Meanwhile, to refresh his memory, he wanted to replay the tapes of Kerslake's interview. The correct procedure had been adhered to, the name and rank of all those present recorded, along with the time and date. Against all advice, Kerslake had refused the services of a solicitor. Ian fast-forwarded the tape and picked it up at the point where the serious questioning began. The suspect's tone was dull but, innocent or guilty, he would have been in a state of shock. As he listened, Ian was able to picture him clearly: a thick-set man of average height, dark brown hair parted on the side and a misshapen nose which had been broken at some point. They were the sort of looks he imagined would appeal to women.

Kerslake claimed to know nothing about the knife or the murder, yet when it was suggested that all the evidence pointed to his guilt and he was asked once more whether he had killed Dee Mercer he had replied, 'It seems as if I must have done,' and, again, later, 'If you say so.' To compound this he had signed a statement which included those remarks and yet, throughout the hours which the interview lasted, he did not change his story concerning his movements.

Ian clicked off the final tape and leant back against the moulded plastic of his chair, arms folded. Kerslake did not look or sound like a murderer, but who really did? Now and then the press managed to unearth photographs of a convicted person which made them look like the psychopath or brute or monster their headlines professed them to be but the majority of killers looked like anybody else. He rubbed his brow between thumb and forefinger, recalling two such people with whom he had dealt – one, a vicar's son, a teenager; another, an old man who had waited years to take his revenge. The overhead fluorescent tube buzzed soothingly and was accompanied by the rhythmic ticking of the clock behind him. The vicar's son and the old man. Their motives were unjustifiable but they were understandable. There was no apparent motive for Dee's murder although, naturally, there was one. If only he could guess what it was – no, he must stop thinking along those lines. It was no longer his problem. But Kelly Mercer was, and it was strange that, during the house-to-house inquiries, no one had mentioned the unusual circumstances of the daughter's disappearance. Kerslake had volunteered that information as he had that of his previous arrest. Perhaps, Ian pondered, these were not the actions of an innocent man wanting everything out in the open before the police had a chance to find out but those of one who was guilty; perhaps it was Kerslake's way of throwing sand in their eyes, trying to prove he had nothing to hide. 'Dammit.' He saw what was happening, he was back on the same track.

'Sir?' One of his younger colleagues interrupted him. 'Derek Cavanagh's on the line.'

'Good. I'll be right there.'

Ian left the interview room he had been using and picked up the nearest extension. With a few brief sentences he informed Cavanagh he would like to talk to him and arranged to see him the following evening.

Back in his own office words from the Kerslake tapes went around and around in his head.

'When did Kelly leave home?' Kerslake had been asked.

'Two, nearly three years ago. In the summer. About six months after I moved in with Dee.'

Ian had replayed this part several times, alert to any nuances. 'Two, nearly three years ago. In the summer.' That had sounded fine. Then a pause. 'About six months after I moved in with Dee.' As if, Ian thought, he had been almost reluctant to add the last phrase. He had gone on to say that he did not know her reasons for going but that Dee had reassured him she was all right. He denied that Kelly might have resented his presence and swore he had no idea where she might be although he had questioned Dee many times. According to Kerslake there had been no Christmas or birthday cards, at least not in Dee's direction. None had been found in the house.

He could hear music as he locked the car and strolled the thirty or so yards home. Ian frowned as he began to suspect it was coming from 14 Belmont Terrace. It was term time, and a weekday, so Mark was not responsible. Besides, on his last visit home his son's musical tastes had not encompassed Ella Fitzgerald. The frown changed to a grin. Doc Harris's tastes did. He hurried up the short narrow path to the front door.

The evenings were drawing out and it was light until almost eight but even so he was amazed to find the patio doors wide open and smoke billowing from their small barbecue. Moira, the Doc and his wife, Shirley, were seated outside with drinks in their hands, albeit wearing jackets or cardigans. 'You're all mad' were his words of greeting. 'Good God, let me move that thing.' He shook his head. Two intelligent women and a qualified doctor and none of them had the sense to place it in a more sheltered position so they would not choke to death.

'It's all my fault,' Shirley admitted. 'The butcher gave us some ribs and sausages and we thought...well...' She raised her hands helplessly as the breeze stirred the shrubs and they all shivered.

Ian poured himself a drink. 'Payment for services rendered?' he asked.

'Not exactly. Shirley looked after the children one day last week.'

'Never again. Not even for a freezerful of fillet steak. I'll help Moira dish up. We'll be eating in the kitchen.'

'That's a relief.'

Tactfully the two women withdrew to allow them a few minutes to talk shop. Doc Harris was their own GP as well as their friend and was on the rota of police surgeons. He was balding and rotund and his fingers were stained brown with nicotine. His usual tipple was a large Scotch. Not a good advertisement for his profession but Ian could not recall him having a day's illness. His first wife had died, a fact about which he was very bitter because he felt he should have been able to save her. However, he had later married Shirley, whom he idolised. Perhaps it was his wife's death which gave birth to his obsession with post-mortems. Although there was no need to, he attended as many as his work permitted, admitting that he wished he had gone in for pathology. His role as a police surgeon was simply to verify death if there were unusual circumstances surrounding it, but mostly he took blood samples and examined prisoners in their cells or victims who, if not seriously injured, were brought straight to the station.

'Ian, what's bothering you? You haven't seemed yourself the last week or so. Isn't it time you took Moira away for a holiday?'

51

'I've got one booked. A fortnight in June, before the schools break up.'

'I'm pleased to hear it. Is it this Kerslake fellow?'

'Yes, dammit.' Ian ran a hand through his hair in exasperation. 'I'm getting as obsessional as you, I can't get it out of my mind.'

'Ob . . . ? Ah, yes. But this is different. The man's awaiting trial. You've done your bit, you've got to let it go or everything else will suffer, including your health.'

'If I could just find the daughter – oh, looks like the food's ready.'

They moved out to the kitchen where most of the Ropers' meals were eaten. Moira would not allow talk of work at the dinner table, including her own. She had recently been promoted to office manager at a local garage which held a franchise for executive model cars and found she got on well with directors and salesmen and mechanics alike.

'Is that mine?' Ian pointed at the shirt she was wearing over a pair of tight-fitting jeans.

'Yes, you don't mind, do you?'

He grinned. 'No. It's rather fetching. Now, before I forget, I shall probably be away tomorrow night. I've got to go to Northampton.' And with the comforting thought that he was to be allowed to continue his inquiries a little longer, he settled down to enjoy the company of his friends.

Ann Proctor spent most evenings in the company of her fiancé, Richie Howlett. Their wedding was planned for the following spring, by which time, they hoped, they would have saved enough for a deposit on a one-bedroomed flat. Because they were saving hard they rarely went out. Some nights they would sit in the Proctors' front room, watching television, but neither of them was particularly comfortable in the pristine surroundings and Eileen would not let Richie smoke in there. Mostly they sat in Richie's bedsit which was a dismal room, one of many in a converted Victorian house in Saxborough Road. The landlord took little interest in the property, other than to collect the rent.

Ann was meticulously careful about taking her contraceptive pills. She wanted the big white wedding which her mother had planned but her father's wrath would be too much to bear if she became pregnant before that date. He was a martinet and his temper was the reason her brother had left home at the first opportunity. Although her mother did not complain and she had not seen any bruises, Ann suspected that her father hit her. Sometimes at night she heard muffled noises from across the landing and instinct told her they were a violent prelude to sex. And now with Dee Mercer's death she was beginning to think that what Kelly had told her might be true.

'Come on, Annie, what's up?' Richie put a finger gently under her chin and raised her head. There were tears in her eyes. She had known him all her life and theirs was a relationship which had grown out of friendship. Since they were fifteen they had been almost inseparable and she would not – could not – marry him without confiding her suspicions. She feared that, straight as he was, he might change his mind about her. On the other hand she would not be able to live with herself if she did not tell him.

'Nothing,' she said, trying to smile.

He decided it was best to leave it. 'Shall we have some cider and watch that video?'

She nodded and settled back into the tatty settee. Her concentration was poor and she lost the thread of the story as she thought about the anomaly which was her father. It was all right for him to eye up the girls in short skirts or revealing tops but he was furious if her mother or herself wore anything other than what he considered to be ladylike. She knew very little about his work in Ipswich, other than that he was in insurance, and she wondered if he ever slept with any of the girls in his office. If this was the case, and her mother had found out, it might account for the strain she was showing. Of course, Dee had been a friend, a close friend. They had coffee together and gossiped and borrowed items of groceries if one or the other ran out because neither had her own car and the nearest shop was quite a walk.

Owen Kerslake had been arrested so that was all right but Ann's one prayer was that the police did not find Kelly. As

53

Richie slipped an arm around her shoulders it struck her that the female detective who had seen her earlier that evening had known she was lying. She knew what she had to do.

'Ian, come on, it's eight thirty.' Moira was shaking his shoulder not too gently and he heard a snort which, he realised, came from the back of his own throat. He had probably been snoring. The Doc was a bad influence when it came to drinking and it had been rather a late night. Out of the corner of his eyes, which he would rather have kept shut, he saw that his wife was fully dressed. She smelled of soap and toothpaste and there was something else; coffee, filter coffee. Groaning, he sat up and saw the mug on the bedside table, steam rising in an unsteady line in the draught from the open window. He hoped the coffee was black.

'It's all right. I'm not expected in until late.'

'You might have told me. Anyway, I'm off now. If I don't hear from you this evening, I'll expect you tomorrow night. I'm going to the cinema with Deirdre.' She leant forward but straightened up without kissing him then said goodbye.

Ian rubbed a hand across his bristled chin. He couldn't blame her, no doubt his breath was none too pleasant. A surfeit of beer and cigarettes did not make for romantic early morning interludes.

Ten minutes later he peered at his sweat-spiked hair in the bathroom mirror. 'Not a pretty sight,' he muttered as he lathered his face prior to shaving. A hot shower would help put things right. He let the water run over his body for a long time then shampooed his hair and scrubbed his teeth.

After a couple of slices of toast and more coffee from the machine which Moira had seen fit to fill, he felt more optimistic. Later he would be seeing Cavanagh. As he sipped the dregs of the coffee he recapped on the previous couple of days' events. A faxed message had been received from Tyneside to the effect that a WPC had interviewed Michelle Short in her hall of residence at Newcastle. Michelle had confirmed that she and Kelly had been close and that she was astonished when she did not return to school in the September. They were both due to start their A level courses in English and history and had made plans to apply to the same universities. 'I saw her once during the first week of the holidays. Nothing seemed to have altered, I mean, she didn't say a word about going away.' It was the same story. Michelle did not know why or where Kelly had gone, but she had added that it was possible they might have started to drift apart because Kelly tended to monopolise her which would have hampered her when it came to making new friendships at university. It was the first time anyone had pointed out even a minor flaw in the girl's character.

'I wrote to her mother to ask for Kelly's address, but I didn't get a reply.'

The only revealing part of the fax came in the final paragraph. Like Pearl Rickman, Michelle Short thought Kelly was close to confiding in her, although she had no idea what about.

Ian rinsed his mug and plate and left them to drain. From the window he watched a mistle thrush land on the bird table before swooping, wings folded back, gracefully to the ground to eat whatever Moira had put out that morning. For a change there were no noisy starlings. He dried his hands and went to fetch his briefcase and car keys.

It was not very warm and there was a damp, low-lying mist but one which, when the sun rose higher, would be burned off. Already he could see the promise of one of those perfect April days when the sky was a clear blue. He set off down the road, leaving the car where it was. For his journey later he would use one of the police pool vehicles.

The rush hour was over and now, at nine thirty, most of the pedestrians were women, some with pre-school-age children. He greeted one or two people he knew but did not stop to chat. The council road sweepers had been and gone, leaving the streets temporarily litter free. From an old-fashioned hairdresser's, where the customers sat under hoods with their hair wound around coloured rollers, a vent in the wall gave off an aroma akin to wet nappies. It made Ian's eyes sting and he wondered how anyone could bear to have a perm. The

55

place, he knew, was only frequented by the more elderly residents of Rickenham Green and the prices were kept proportionately low.

The Ipswich double-decker pulled in and Ian had to wait to cross the road until the queue had boarded.

He turned down a side road, came out by the Town Hall and continued for the short distance to the station. The reception area was unusually quiet. There was almost a Sunday afternoon feeling. It obviously suited the desk sergeant who hastily thrust a copy of the *Sun* beneath the counter when he saw Ian's large frame filling one section of the revolving doors.

Ian nodded and said good morning then went on up to his office where he consulted a map and calculated how long to allow for his journey. He would join the A45 at Stowmarket, bypass Cambridge then continue along the A604 as far as Wellingborough. From there he would go cross-country to Oddlesham. It was not a town he knew and he anticipated a night away with pleasure. If he timed it right he could stop for something to eat on the way.

Derek Cavanagh had been puzzled as to why the Rickenham police wanted to question him but Ian had given him no clues. Logically, it would have been far simpler just to ask if he knew where Kelly was or even if she was living with him but Ian suspected there was something suspicious about his leaving the comprehensive in the manner he had and wanted the element of surprise on his side. And, as Superintendent Thorne had agreed, a face-to-face interview was far more satisfactory as the reactions to certain questions could not be so easily disguised.

He had been warned that the accounts department could not be expected to foot the bill, although his petrol and sustenance expenses would be reimbursed. Therefore, no four star hotel but, he grinned, hopefully, a comfortable inn which served real ale. He rummaged in the bottom drawer of his desk and found an old copy of the *Good Beer Guide*. The up-to-date copy Mark had bought him for Christmas was at home. As he made the call he wondered how he could possibly be thinking of beer after last night's excesses but, as much as he loved Adnam's bitter, it would make a pleasant change to sample some Tetley's or Marston's Pedigree. He made a reservation then grunted. What was the point in having local bitters when the trend was for pubs to have guest beers? He disliked the fact that you could buy almost anything anywhere then admitted that, as he grew older, there were more and more things about the modern world he did not like.

Having tidied up a few loose ends he checked with Gina that nothing urgent required his attention and told her to expect him in the day after tomorrow.

'But – oh, I forgot. Tomorrow's your day off. Have a good time.' She wished him a safe journey then bet herself a month's salary that the Chief would put in an appearance at some point the following day even if it was an official day off. Something was bothering him and when it did he was like a terrier with a bone until he found a resolution.

Ian listened to the radio as he drove, stopping once to refill the petrol tank. As he slipped a credit card beneath the glass security partition he saw the bars of chocolate behind the cashier and purchased one. Eating it as he continued on his route he realised he would not need to eat again before he saw Cavanagh so headed straight for the pub in Oddlesham where he was more than satisfied with his accommodation. The room was *en suite* and there was a television and tea and coffee-making facilities. It seemed that everywhere now offered what had once been available only at grand hotels. Because he was early he made tea and lay on the bed watching a quiz programme, feeling decadent to be watching television at that time of day. From the town street map which was pinned to the wall in the corridor between the bar and the stairs he saw that it was less than a ten-minute walk to where Cavanagh lived.

At five forty-five he washed his face, put on his jacket and went out into the unfamiliar streets.

Markham had been sent to see Owen Kerslake, this time in the presence of Victor Rowland. He had been asked about Kelly after his arrest but this time the questions would be more searching. It seemed impossible that Kerslake, having lived under the same roof as the girl, if only for six months, had no inkling as to what had become of her.

Markham knew well enough that he must avoid the subject of Dee's murder but if anything had happened to Kelly, it would be a different crime.

'I'm not a liar,' Kerslake stated calmly and quietly and, Markham thought, with dignity. 'It was the one secret Dee kept from me and, to this day, I have absolutely no idea why. I liked Kelly but I loved her mother. If she had reasons for not telling anyone where Kelly went, then they have died with her, but I have never doubted her integrity.'

Markham nodded and left it at that. As he stood up to leave he caught Victor Rowland's eye and they exchanged a look which suggested both men believed Kerslake to be telling the truth.

'Can you spare me a minute?' Rowland also stood and picked up his bulky leather case. Outside in the corridor he said, 'I don't expect an explicit answer, but I don't suppose any more evidence has come to light?'

Markham stared at him, his blue eyes hard. Solicitors and the police were not renowned for friendly co-operation but this man he had time for. 'Look, we're trying to find the girl, the rest is down to you and Kerslake's mouthpiece when it comes to trial.'

'Thanks.' Victor Rowland grinned, showing a row of imperfect teeth. He had come across Markham before and had not expected a civil answer let alone one which told him so much. 'See you around.'

But Markham was already striding away, his hands in the pockets of his leather jacket.

Why, he thought, just as Ian and everyone who had heard the tapes had done, why did Kerslake make that stupid comment? During the first half-hour of the interview, when asked if he had killed his wife, he had said, 'I suppose I must have done.' Shock, maybe, or confusion, or guilt. Had they got the wrong man? It happened, of course, but they had been so thorough. And why had Kerslake waited for more than forty-five minutes before ringing them? Markham wondered if this was to give himself time to destroy any damning evidence. Even so, there had been blood on the sole of one shoe despite his claim he had not set foot inside the kitchen. He shrugged. Kelly Mercer was now their concern, not her mother's boyfriend.

Brenda Gibbons continued to work her way through the list of youths who had shared Pat Reynolds as their year tutor, but only when it did not interfere with other work. She also decided to make a few tentative inquiries about the members of staff who had left during that period, excluding Cavanagh whom the Chief was seeing personally.

Angela Clarke had retired but still lived in her bungalow in Little Endesley. One telephone call informed Brenda that she had not come into contact with Kelly since she was in her first year at the comprehensive and until she had read of the awful events in the *Rickenham Herald* had had no idea what had become of the girl. 'I couldn't tell you,' she had said in response to DC Gibbons's question concerning Kelly's future. 'It's eight years since I taught her. If I recall correctly, she was a promising pupil, but by the time they're fourteen they often change. No, I didn't know she was going to stay on.'

Brenda established that Angela Clarke lived alone and had no intention of moving, although why she did so she was not sure, but it did eliminate her from the inquiry. Later she would try and locate Maggie Simpson.

Derek Cavanagh had been shaken when one of the school secretaries had told him that Detective Chief Inspector Roper, from Rickenham Green CID, wished to speak to him. He had been in a class when the call came. He returned the call but was still no wiser as to why the man wished to see him when he had hung up. However, he complied with the request because he was tired of running. Naturally he did not want the police arriving at the school so he had agreed readily to being seen at his home. It must be important if an officer of that rank

59

was paying a personal visit otherwise they would have sent someone from the local force. It might have been problematic if Jenny was around but that evening she would be driving the girls to Brownies, the hall where their pack met being two miles away. Better still, she always spent the intervening time with the mother of another Brownie before she went back to collect them.

Derek had arrived home just after four thirty and the hour and a quarter until his family departed seemed interminable. At last he kissed his wife and daughters and waved as they drove off. He stood by the window watching for an unknown car to pull up and was flustered when the man arrived on foot. He had opened the door before his visitor had had time to knock.

Ian had approached the house slowly because his walk had taken less time than he had anticipated. Also, he wanted to gain an impression of the area in which Cavanagh lived. The street consisted of turn-of-the-century buildings. They were solidly built but had little else to recommend them; Ian supposed they were in keeping with what a scale 2 teacher could afford. The street may have been uninspiring but at least no one had put leaded panes in their windows or tried to make the houses into anything other than what they were.

His hand was half raised to ring the bell when the door opened. 'Chief Inspector Roper?'

'Yes. Hello.' He extended his hand. Ian's first thought was that if there had been, or still was, anything between Cavanagh and Kelly Mercer it was perfectly understandable. Judging by her photographs Kelly was not only young, but beautiful; Derek Cavanagh was the best-looking man Ian had ever set eyes upon. Marginally shorter than himself, he had thick hair which was almost black. It was cut in a modern style and accentuated his strong, lean features, his sensuous mouth and the Mediterranean tone of his skin. It was not tanned but more suggestive of Spanish or Italian ancestors.

'Won't you come in? My wife's out, by the way, I take it you didn't need to speak to her?'

'No, I don't think that'll be necessary.' Wife. Ian's mind was

60

working rapidly. The word might be a euphemism; Cavanagh could have married Kelly by now, enough time had elapsed to get a divorce, or he had been badly mistaken. Convenient that she happened not to be at home, he thought, as he was shown into the lounge.

'Can I get you something? A drink perhaps?' Cavanagh waved a hand towards a tray on which were several bottles. Ian declined the offer. 'Then, please, do sit down.'

The three-piece suite was covered in a greyish-blue velveteen and was comfortable. Ian sat back and crossed his long legs, trying to assess whether his host was agitated because of his presence or for some other reason.

'I have no idea what this is all about.' He gave a weak grin. 'I haven't set foot in Rickenham for nearly three years so it can't be a driving offence.'

'No.' He came straight to the point. 'We're trying to locate Kelly Mercer.'

'Good heavens. And you think I know what's happened to her?'

'*Has* something happened to her?'

Heat rose in Cavanagh's face. 'I didn't mean it the way it sounded. I assumed that by now she'd be at college or university somewhere.'

'She didn't go back to school. She disappeared during the summer holidays when you left Rickenham.'

'Disappeared? I don't understand what you mean.' He frowned. 'If that's so, why have you waited all this time to try to find her?'

'Because we didn't know. Look, I find it hard to believe you don't know about her mother.'

'Of course I do, I read about it, but what's this got to do with Kelly? God, I sound stupid. Apart from what it's done to her, that is.'

'Kelly went missing in 1993. No one has heard of her or from her since and she didn't turn up for her mother's funeral. Now, what can you tell me about the girl?'

'Oh, this is ridiculous. It's three years ago, I've taught hundreds of children, I can't remember anything that might be relevant.'

61

'I would've thought you'd recall a girl you taught during your last year at Rickenham Comprehensive, especially one who was doing so well.' Ian took a chance. 'Or is it that you're one of those teachers to whom pupils are nothing more than statistics, you know, get them through their exams and more power to your elbow?'

'Of course not. I take my job seriously. You've got it all wrong, I simply don't think about Rickenham, I just wanted to put it all behind me.'

And now we're getting somewhere, Ian thought. 'May I ask why?'

Cavanagh glanced nervously at the clock which stood between some books on a shelf. His body seemed to slump. 'I don't suppose you'll go until you've satisfied your prurient curiosity.' He noticed the Chief Inspector's brows narrow. The arrow had struck home. He took a deep breath, unwilling to speak the words. 'My wife was having an affair with a colleague, a man I had considered to be my friend.'

'Your wife?'

'Yes, that's what I said.'

There was silence for several seconds as Ian digested this piece of information. Not the handsome Cavanagh and Kelly, but his wife. How foolish he had been, the idea had not even occurred to him. This, then, was the personal reason which had caused him to leave the area and had given Ian a wasted journey. 'I'm sorry.' It was the best he could come up with.

'Not as sorry as I was.' Cavanagh's voice was low and full of bitterness. 'God, what a cliché, my wife and my best friend. I couldn't have stayed, not for anything. We talked it over and Jenny agreed to make a new start. And now this.' He placed his elbows on the arms of his chair and held his head between his fingertips.

If it was Cavanagh's wife who had been unfaithful it proved the old adage that looks were not everything. Ian decided to throw in the towel and get a few pints of Tetley's down him before finding somewhere to get a curry. For once he was grateful that the accounts department were not footing the bill for his accommodation; he would have had a lot of questions to answer to justify the expense. After he'd eaten he would enjoy the privilege of being a guest of the inn and have a couple of nightcaps and tomorrow, what bliss, a full English breakfast followed by a leisurely drive home. As he made a move to get up he asked, this time with genuine prurient curiosity, 'Do male staff in mixed sex schools encounter many problems with the girls? Sixth-formers, I mean?'

Now that the danger had passed and the DCI seemed to be leaving before Jenny was due back, Cavanagh was prepared to be lightly humorous. 'If you want to know whether they throw their knickers at us in droves, then no. Most of them treat us like aliens. Only rarely does a girl try to flirt and that's usually at the instigation of her classmates and more often than not a joke.'

'Has it ever happened to you?'

Cavanagh relaxed as he saw his visitor stand up and button his jacket. 'Not really and if it had there was no way I would have risked either my marriage or my job. Ironic, isn't it?'

'Thank you, Mr Cavanagh, I'm sorry to have wasted your time.'

Cavanagh had opened the lounge door and stepped back to let Ian pass, almost bumping into him as Ian asked, 'One more thing, what was Kelly like? As a person, I mean, not as a student?'

'She always tried hard to please, not just by doing well with her school work, but in all sorts of ways, and she lacked that edge some of them had, she wasn't spiteful. I'd go as far as to say her personality matched her looks. She was almost angelic. But I always felt there was something underneath it all, something she managed to keep hidden from everybody.'

'But you didn't ask,' Ian stated, not expecting a response.

'Goodness, no. It's best for a male member of staff not to get involved in the girls' personal problems and she had her year tutor in whom to confide. Don't get me wrong, you get to know a bit about their background, but with girls of that age you have to be careful. Maybe it was boyfriend trouble, she was a beautiful girl. Kelly – '

Both men jumped when the door behind them which led to the kitchen was flung open and crashed into the hall wall. 'So Kelly Mercer's still with us, is she?'

All Ian was aware of for several seconds was the clatter of feet as two small girls raced up the stairs and a young woman with a pretty, but tired face and a slender figure who stood staring at her husband accusingly.

As Jennifer Cavanagh followed her daughters upstairs Ian said a silent goodbye to his curry but hoped there would be time for a couple of drinks. Before then he needed to find out a few things. What the hell is going on in the Cavanagh household, he wondered, as he indicated the lounge door with a movement of his head.

Cavanagh sighed, opened it, and led his guest in for the second time.

6

Michelle Short had decided that she would move into digs during her second year as a student at Newcastle but for the time being her room in one of the halls of residence had to suffice. It was on a par with most such accommodation, being rectangular and cramped and possessing a narrow bed which did nothing to hinder the sexual activity of her neighbour whose every groan and gasp she could hear through the thin partition which acted as a wall. There was a wash-basin and a built-in desk over which was a shelf for books. She had provided her own reading lamp and a few posters.

She sat on the hard edge of her bed, unable to concentrate on what she was supposed to be studying. The visit from the WPC had unnerved her. How stupid they had been; herself, Kelly and Lizzie Conrad. On her last visit home she had learned that Lizzie was still at the Duke of Clarence and was well on her way to being made up to head receptionist. She would go far, as Michelle herself intended to. As long as the past did not interfere.

How strange that Kelly, the mildest of them all, should have suddenly shown a wild streak.

Michelle stood up and paced the tiny room. In the mirror over the basin she caught a glimpse of her flushed face. She took for granted her slim figure and her dark curly hair and blue eyes which attracted men. Not quite in Kelly's league, she was nevertheless perfectly satisfied with the way she looked, but this had not induced vanity.

Dee Mercer was dead. Murdered, and by her lover. It had come as a shock and upset her far more than she would have imagined. Dee was – had been – a nice woman, one who always made the best of everything. The bigger shock had come from the WPC who had told her Kelly had not gone home for the funeral. Michelle had not liked lying to her but she had her own future to consider.

Knowing it would be a waste of time to try to continue studying she brushed her hair, put on some lipstick and made her way to the union bar to seek some distraction.

'You must eat or you'll make yourself ill.' Eileen Proctor frowned as she watched her daughter pushing food around her plate. It was the second evening in a row Ann had claimed she was not hungry.

Eileen was a tall, raw-boned woman who had once been as attractive as Ann but whose auburn hair was now streaked with paler strands and whose face bore the lines of unhappiness. Apart from Sean, who had some mysterious hold over her, Ann was the only person about whom she cared and she could not bear to see her miserable. 'Is it Richie, love? Have you had a quarrel?'

'No.'

'What is it then?'

Ann shook her head. 'I don't know. Pre-wedding nerves, I expect.'

Eileen sighed and picked up the plate from which she scraped the half-eaten meal into the bin. It was far too early for pre-wedding nerves, it wasn't for another year. Did Ann suspect something? Did she know what Eileen knew? She shook her head. Best not to think about it but to carry on as normal. All she cared about was the family.

They were standing at the bar of the Feathers discussing the case, but as the pub began to fill up they moved to their usual corner where their privacy would not be invaded. DC Brenda Gibbons summed up their various comments. 'Three years ago she ups and vanishes and not one single person we have spoken to has any idea where or why. Something's wrong, it has to be.'

Between them they had seen or spoken to most of her class-mates and the general consensus, even from those who barely knew the girl, was that she was 'nice' or 'friendly'. 'If I hear the word nice once more I think I'm going to scream.'

'How can you stand that stuff?' DS Barry Swan nodded at her glass. It contained Campari and soda, which was Brenda's favourite drink. 'It's like medicine.'

'Acts like it, too, after a long day,' she retorted. 'Anyway, why're you so bad-tempered? Sorry, I shouldn't have said that.' She looked away, embarrassed, as Barry and the Chief exchanged a look whose meaning she could not decipher but which told her there was something only the two of them knew about.

'What do you make of our missing angel?' DC Campbell asked in order to come to Brenda's aid.

Markham shrugged. Nice, not nice, he didn't care. His job was to help to find her.

'You're as voluble as ever,' Brenda said, quite recovered, when Markham did not reply. 'Are we here for the duration?'

'I'm in no hurry, Moira's out. Again,' Ian added with heavy undertones. 'I don't know about the rest of you.'

'I'm game.' This from Alan Campbell.

'Not me, I'm going home.' Barry finished his lager and placed his glass on the table. No one commented and no one tried to persuade him to stay. He had been distracted for the last couple of days and they were beginning to think they knew what was worrying him although no one had voiced their thoughts. Barry had confided in Ian the morning after

Lucy had told him the news. Ian, too, had been hesitant about offering congratulations and had simply said he hoped everything would turn out all right this time. He knew Barry would not relax until Lucy's pregnancy had passed the stage where she had previously fallen.

'Do you suppose that Kerslake could've been set up? Or could the "nice" daughter have popped home and knocked her mother off? I don't understand it, except when two people live under the same roof there's always a possible motive.'

Brenda and the Chief stared at one another. Markham, a man of so few words, had not only uttered three consecutive sentences but had added a touch of philosophy. But what he said made sense. Kelly Mercer might not be a victim but a murderer, hence the reason for keeping her head down. But if Kerslake had been set up, why, and by whom?

'Tell me, Markham,' Brenda asked with more than a touch of acerbity, 'how come you're suddenly an expert on living together?' Markham may have indulged in the occasional one night stand but to their knowledge he had never taken a girl back to his own flat.

'Oh, for God's sake. Why can't everyone stop bickering?' Ian snapped.

'Sorry, sir.' It was typical of Alan Campbell that he took the responsibility of apologising for them all upon his own shoulders.

'Yes, well, none of us is at our best. I just don't know what to make of it. Guilty or not Kerslake has been involved in two incidents which involved young girls – the one he was alleged to have had sexual intercourse with and then Kelly's disappearance – and now, knowing what we do about young Kelly, well . . .' He raised his hands in despair. The girl seemed to have been leading a double life, one in which it was not beyond the bounds of possibility that she had left herself open to blackmail or murder. 'We've got another week as far as the Super's concerned. So keep looking.' Ian drained his glass. He had fancied a night in the pub with his colleagues but the idea no longer appealed. 'I'm off, I'll see you tomorrow.' He ground the stub of his cigarette into an almost full ashtray and walked out, ducking to avoid the central beam across the ceiling.

There were nights when they assembled in one of the pubs, when a case was going badly or when one was over. They would stand and discuss it as a form of therapy, a way of getting it out of their systems before going home to their families or throwing themselves into something else. Mostly, of course, their cases were not in isolation, they were usually in the middle of several at once.

Alan Campbell was tempted to remain but knew his limitations. He could not drink as much as the others and he had no intention of allowing them to see him drunk. He, too, said his goodnights although he was vaguely jealous that this would leave Brenda and Markham together.

'Thanks a bunch,' Brenda commented when, to her surprise, Markham turned abruptly and said there was someone he had to see. She stood at the bar smiling cynically. They couldn't accuse her of not lasting the pace.

'Can I get you another?'

She frowned and turned to her left, her usual response of 'Bugger off' stifled as she bit her lip. She recognised the tall, lean man with the pock-marked face as a partner in a firm of solicitors with which she had had professional dealings. He was not at all good-looking but she was more attracted to the unusual than to the handsome. She grinned, giving him the full benefit of her generous mouth and even teeth. 'Well, why not?' she said.

Andrew Osborne's eyes widened in surprise before he grinned back. It was not the answer he had been expecting. 'Same again?' Brenda nodded and he picked up her glass and headed towards the bar. She watched his retreating back and wondered if he played tennis.

Superintendent Thorne knew it was nearing the time when he had to put a stop to it. Just because there was no body did not mean that Kelly Mercer was still alive but there was no evidence pointing to her death either. He suspected she might have simply dropped out of society and be living in a city earning her living in the way such girls did. The funeral was over now. Kelly had still not shown up. Understandable if she and her mother had not been on good terms but everyone they had spoken to seemed to think they had been. 'Okay, Ian, another couple of days and that's it. Get on to this Simpson woman and leave it at that. Did you follow up Cavanagh's story?'

'Yes. Looks like he's telling the truth.'

'Looks like?'

'Well, there's no one to corroborate it but it all fits. His wife was trying to make him look bad in my eyes because she was protecting her own back.'

'Is that the time?' Mike Thorne glanced at the clock and reached for his jacket simultaneously. 'I've got a meeting in ten minutes. I'll leave it with you, Ian.'

Ian walked the length of the corridor with him and gave a brief wave as Thorne hurried down the stairs. He pushed open the door of his own office. It smelled of stale smoke. He opened the window a couple of inches but it did not stop him lighting another cigarette. He was at the point where he had decided to give up again but during those periods he smoked more than ever as if he was trying to build up his nicotine level for the torture which lay ahead.

For several minutes he sat staring at the wall. He was going over the evening he had spent at Cavanagh's house and what had followed. Naturally he had wanted to know what his wife meant with her remark about Kelly still being with them. Painfully, Cavanagh had explained.

'I asked Jenny to take one of my jackets to the cleaners,' he had said. 'I didn't empty the pockets, I had nothing to hide. Only I'd forgotten something.' There had been a long pause as he assessed whether or not DCI Roper would believe him. 'I hadn't worn the jacket for a while, not since the previous term, in fact. I'd forgotten about the photograph. It was of Kelly. She was wearing very little and was posed provocatively.'

'What do you mean by very little?' Ian had asked.

'A pair of knickers. And you want to know how I came by it. Whatever I say is going to sound feeble, but you have to

69

believe it's the truth. Kelly was in the corridor at school when a group of third-year boys went crashing past. I yelled at them, they're not supposed to run in the corridors, but she'd dropped her bag and the contents were all over the floor. I bent down to help her pick them up and that's when I found the picture.'

'She had it in her own possession?' It had puzzled Ian as to why she would be carrying it around on school premises.

'Yes. I asked if there were any more. She was desperately embarrassed and said there weren't but she refused to tell me who had taken it. I was extremely concerned, she was fifteen at the time. I confiscated it, keeping it in my pocket so it couldn't fall into other hands. For three or four days I debated whether I ought to tell Pat Reynolds or even the head. I don't know how or why I came to the decision, perhaps it was cowardly, but I decided to say nothing. I thought she might have learned her lesson, that she'd think I *had* told someone else. In retrospect it sounds so pathetic. The weather changed and I didn't wear the jacket again and then Jenny found the photograph. A month or so later, quite inadvertently, I found out about the affair. She tried to convince me that if I hadn't been screwing schoolgirls, her words, not mine, it would never have happened. However, I later found out from John, that was the man she was seeing, that it had been going on for several years. Jenny did use the photo as an excuse but I think when she found it she genuinely believed the worst. So you see, there was more than one reason why we needed a new start.'

Having missed out on a curry Ian had returned to the pub where he was staying and had a couple of drinks before going to bed. The landlord obligingly made him some sandwiches which he took to his room. The following morning he had gone to the school where Cavanagh now taught and had spoken to the headmaster and Cavanagh's colleagues. The man was liked and trusted and considered to be a good teacher. Despite the weakness of his story, Ian believed he was telling the truth. Either way, it showed a different side to Kelly Mercer from the one they had already seen.

But even if he seduced the whole of the fifth year, Ian

thought, it doesn't get us any nearer to finding the girl. He decided to talk it over with Moira.

'I thought you said she didn't have any boyfriends.' Moira peered into the oven from which came the smell of garlic. Ian studied the curves of her buttocks as the material of her skirt stretched over them. When she stood up her face was flushed and a wisp of hair had escaped from the band which held it back on the nape of her neck.

'That's what we were led to believe. However, Cavanagh claims Kelly refused to say anything other than that it was a boyfriend.'

'Ian . . .' Moira chewed the skin around her thumbnail. 'Doesn't it strike you as odd?' He had begun to discuss Kerslake with her, as he did any case which bothered him. She could be trusted implicitly not to repeat anything he said. 'The other time, when Owen Kerslake was arrested, the girl involved said it was him who had taken the picture to protect her boyfriend – maybe Cavanagh's using a non-existent boyfriend to protect himself. And if that's so and Kelly was about to spill the beans, he might have had to silence her.'

Ian groaned. He had been thinking along those lines too. 'This is getting completely out of hand. We've got two men who have managed to get themselves into trouble – trouble, I hasten to add, which involves under-age girls – and, God help me, I believe them both. And before you say anything, it's nothing to do with the fact that I'm a man, and you know I don't hold sexist views.'

Moira raised her eyes to the ceiling and made an exclamation that sounded like 'Ha!' Ian was hurt. He tried very hard not to, but his wife obviously did not think he had succeeded.

'There's another way of looking at it, of course.' Ian waited. If she came out with a sensible suggestion he would forgive her for the scornful laugh. 'Kerslake may have taken all the pictures.'

It fitted. It fitted very neatly. He had admitted to being alone in the house with the first girl and must have had numerous opportunities to be alone with Kelly, and in the latter's case it

71

would be a reasonable explanation for her disappearance. 'One thing doesn't fit though.'

Moira pushed his elbow out of the way as she began to lay the table. 'What's that?'

'If you're right, why didn't Dee Mercer make a fuss when Kelly disappeared?'

'Either because Kelly gave her some other explanation as to why she had suddenly changed her mind about her future, or else she knew.'

'Come off it.'

'No, Ian, it's not impossible. If Dee loved him as much as people seem to think, she might have done anything to keep him, including sending Kelly away. That would also explain why she wouldn't tell him where she was. Now put the radio on and let's have some cheerful entertainment.'

Ian did so then sat down to enjoy his meal. The workings of a woman's mind were far more devious than a man's, he thought. Not for the first time he was glad he did not have a daughter.

7

A draw would have sufficed but Norwich City, the Canaries, had managed to concede a goal in injury time. Ian began to think he should have listened to his son's advice and followed Ipswich which was, after all, his local team. But he couldn't help it. For some unknown reason he had supported Norwich since he was seven years old and he could not change allegiance now. It was typical that they should lose one of the few matches he was able to attend.

Moira had seen by his face when he returned that evening that there would be little conversation. She found it hard to understand how a grown man could brood for hours over something which, to her, was so utterly trivial. Once, in their early days, she had gone to a match with him, thinking they might share their hobbies, but she was ready to leave by half-time.

72

'There's always next week,' she told him cheerfully as she handed him a glass of beer. His glare warned her to leave the subject alone so she went into the other room to continue with some dressmaking.

It rained all day on Sunday which did nothing to improve Ian's mood. They had planned a day at the coast with a long walk: that was Moira's idea, then a pub lunch. Instead Moira did the ironing in the kitchen and listened to the radio while Ian watched sport on the television.

The rain was soft and fine, the sort which seemed harmless but was able to penetrate through layers of clothing. It had not ceased by Monday morning. Consequently the traffic was heavier than usual. By the time he arrived at the station Ian was ready to snap at anyone. There had been no telephone calls over the weekend to inform him that Kelly Mercer had been found.

'What is it?' DC Gibbons, looking crisp and fresh and smelling faintly of something flowery, was waiting to see him. Her clear skin and shining hair made him feel old.

'I've been thinking, sir,' she replied, ignoring his gruffness. 'You see, I was speaking to Andrew Osborne the other night and he . . .'

'Andrew Osborne?' Ian interrupted. He had no idea what she was talking about.

'He's a partner with Franklin, Osborne and Potts.'

'Oh, that shower.'

'Yes. Well, anyway, he was asking if I knew who represented Dee Mercer.'

'Bloody ambulance chaser. I'm surprised he didn't get on to it sooner.' Ian turned to open the window. For some reason the radiators were being left on overnight. Someone would get their knuckles rapped because the powers that be normally insisted they were all turned off long before winter was really over.

'Coffee, sir?' Gina, from her office two doors away, had heard his arrival and sensed that he needed sweetening up.

'Thanks. Brenda?'

'Please.' She was used to the Chief's moods and sensibly ignored them. 'We weren't discussing the case *per se*. Andrew

73

simply pointed out that he had heard that Archibald, Durham and Co. were involved. He'd read in the *Herald* we were looking for Kelly and he supposed they would be too, as she's the beneficiary. It stands to reason that they'll make the usual appeals in newspapers much as we've been doing.' She wanted to make clear that there had been no breach of professional conduct on either side.

'Very noble of Mr Osborne, but don't you think he might have a vested interest of his own?'

'Sir?'

'It can't be every day that that ugly brute gets the chance to hold a conversation with an attractive woman.' Just in time Ian saw the angry flush rise in Brenda's face. 'Forgive me, I'm sorry. That was totally uncalled for.' His comment was both unfair and too personal and it wouldn't surprise him if, behind his back, people said much the same about himself and Moira. But his outburst had dispelled his gloominess. 'Ah, here's the coffee. Thanks, Gina.'

Gina grinned at Brenda and raised her shoulders in a gesture which indicated she, too, found the Chief's moods hard to cope with.

'I think I can see what you're getting at, Brenda. If the solicitors are advertising, especially along the lines of – what do they say? Hearing something to your advantage or some such ridiculous phrase – it makes it even more likely that something's happened to Kelly. Few people could resist making contact.'

'Precisely.' Brenda sipped her coffee. It was instant and too milky and obviously a cheap brand. 'Unless, of course, Kelly does know but is aware that her mother had little to leave her.'

'What was the total amount?'

'Altogether, about eleven hundred pounds.'

'If I was nineteen or twenty I wouldn't turn my nose up at that amount.'

'I wouldn't now, sir.'

They drank their coffee in silence. 'It's Dee's mother I feel sorry for. You don't expect to outlive your children nor to have a granddaughter go missing.'

74

'No. Anyway, I'd better get on with things.' Brenda placed her cup and saucer on the desk, stood up and swung her hair over her shoulders, and left the Chief to his own thoughts.

The grandmother. Was it worth him paying her another visit? She lived in an adapted bungalow on the outskirts of Rickenham and spent her days in a wheelchair. The progressive neurological disease from which she suffered meant she experienced long stretches in hospital when the disability was at its worst. She had been unable to attend the funeral because she was hospitalised at the time. They knew Dee had been a conscientious daughter and had paid regular visits to her mother but how close had Mrs Mercer been to her granddaughter?

Ian sighed. He did not know why he was so irascible lately. Moira tried to jolly him out of it by saying he was going through a mid-life crisis, whatever that was supposed to mean. He suspected it was more to do with seeing young, keen officers like Brenda Gibbons working their way through the ranks. He was certainly more aware of his own mortality. Even Barry Swan, who had once been a young, irritating upstart, had matured and married and was developing lines around his eyes.

What worried him more was his obsession with Owen Kerslake's innocence. He did not want to believe that all he was trying to do was to prove that he had not lost his touch and that experience counted for more than youth and ambition and the honours degrees with which some of them leapfrogged the ranks.

He went downstairs to head the morning's briefing then, for want of something better to do, he decided to go and see Mrs Mercer. He telephoned the bungalow first to ascertain she was at home and not at the hospital. She agreed to see him immediately and sounded glad of the chance of some company.

It was a little after nine thirty. The morning's briefing had been short. DC Gibbons was beginning to make headway on the robberies and was to continue working on them, and everyone else was given their instructions. Barry Swan was to see Ann Proctor regarding Maggie Simpson whom, Ian was adamant, he wanted found. So far all they knew was that she had left the school during Kelly's last year but earlier, at the end of the term before the Easter holidays. No one at the school knew where she had gone and she had not returned to teaching. As she was unmarried she had not gone because of a husband's transfer. All the other members of staff had by now been eliminated.

Miss Margaret Simpson was a young woman, in her thirties, and had taught history, but she had not been responsible for Kelly's education after the third year. Jean Adams, the headmistress, had said that she had left unexpectedly. 'Oh, don't get me wrong, she gave us the requisite amount of notice, but I rather thought she was happy here. In fact, it was on the cards that she was going to apply for the position of head of department,' she had told Ian when he telephoned her once more. 'There was no question of a reference. Out of the blue she stated that she didn't think she was suited to teaching and was going to try something new, although she did not stipulate what that might be.'

The only reason that Ian believed it worth sending Barry to speak to Ann was that the girl's school records showed the only time she had done really well was under the aegis of Maggie Simpson.

DS Swan rang his wife at the bank where she worked in the loans department and said he would be home late. 'I've got to see someone on my way back but it shouldn't take too long.' In the background he heard other voices and the hum of machinery. 'Are you okay?'

'Of course I am.'

He pictured her in her grey suit and white blouse, although she'd have probably removed the jacket, with her brown hair brushing her shoulders. She had had it trimmed recently and it suited her better than when it was longer. Best of all he liked it when she pinned it up. He ran a hand through his own fair hair and hoped he would not lose any more of it. He was vain, but not so vain as to resort to doing anything about it if he did.

They had agreed that Ann Proctor should not be warned that Barry was coming. He would go over to Culver Road about six thirty and hope that it wasn't one of her late nights on the till. If it was he would have to return and hope that her parents had not got in touch with her.

As it happened he need not have waited until the evening because it was Ann's day off.

The door was answered by a burly, thick-set man to whom, for no particular reason, Barry took an instant dislike. His smarmy manner did nothing to help. 'Ah, our wonderful guardians of the peace are here again. You seem to like it in Culver Road. You'd better come in.' He held the door wide open and made a sweeping gesture with his hand. 'How can we help you this time?'

'It's your daughter I've come to see.'

'Ann?' The gingery eyebrows drew together and Sean Proctor's mouth tightened. 'What for? My daughter's a good girl.'

'I only want to clarify a couple of things.' Barry refused to allow the man to annoy him.

'Who is it, dear?' Eileen came down the stairs with a towel wrapped around her head. She was in a dressing-gown and was in the middle of getting ready to go out.

'The police. Again,' he added pointedly. 'He wants to see Ann.'

'She's in her room, I'll fetch her.'

'You can wait in there.' Proctor indicated a door off the hall-way but did not open it, retiring instead to the kitchen.

My God, Barry thought when he entered the room. It was like a museum. On a hot day they must stick to the plastic covers. He heard a noise and looked up. Ann Proctor was standing in the doorway. Her face was pale but he was taken aback at her beauty. Yes, he thought, beauty. She had the sort of looks girls usually grew into when they reached their late twenties. Her face would not have been out of place on the cover of *Vogue*. 'Hello, I'm Detective Sergeant Swan.' She seemed frightened and he tried to put her at ease. 'There's nothing to worry about, I just need to ask you a couple of questions. Is that all right with you?' There was no response. Ann stood with her hands clasped together in front of her as if she was trying to control their movements. 'We still haven't been able to find Kelly so we're speaking to all her old teachers. We thought you might be able to help.'

'I told that other one, I don't know anything about Kelly.'

'No, but you do remember Miss Simpson, Maggie Simpson?'

'Of course I do, she used to teach me history.' Her tone registered surprise at the question but she seemed to relax a little. She was on safer ground now. Footsteps passed the door and continued on up the stairs. Ann had hoped her mother might come to her rescue.

'Miss Simpson left the school. From all accounts she was a very good teacher but she suddenly decided she wasn't cut out for the job. I wonder why that might be?'

'Because she . . . well, I expect she got fed up with the kids.'

Bull's-eye, Barry thought. She knows something. 'You got on well with her, didn't you?'

'Most of the girls did. We were supposed to go to our year tutor if we had problems, but nearly everyone went to her after they'd been in her class.'

'I see. She sounds a very understanding lady.'

'Oh, she was, she . . .' but once again Ann stopped short.

'You did exceptionally well in her class, was that because you liked her so much?' Barry watched for her reaction. She jerked slightly. He was satisfied. The full implication of what he had said had sunk in. If she realised they had delved into her own background she would start wondering just how much more they knew.

'Yes, and because, like you said, she was a good teacher.'

'And would you have any idea where she went?'

'Why should I have?'

Barry smiled and brushed back his hair. Why indeed? 'No reason, I just thought it was possible she may have mentioned her plans to someone she was so obviously fond of.'

There was another silence which was soon filled by the sound of a hair-drier. Outside a car door slammed. 'Don't the school know?'

Barry hesitated, then said, 'We'll check.' They had and they didn't. 'Well, if you can't help . . .' It was his turn to leave a sentence unfinished. She could infer whatever she liked.

At the front door Barry reminded her to telephone if there was anything she did remember.

'I . . .' Another pause.

'Yes?' He stepped outside, not wishing to appear too eager.

'She once said something about a farmhouse. She had plans for it. It's somewhere in Norfolk.' And before Barry could say another word she had closed the door in his face.

He strolled back to the car where two boys were, he hoped, only admiring it. Their guilty faces suggested they may have been thinking of something other than stroking the polished paintwork of the sports model and the way they stood, hands in pockets, scuffing their feet and avoiding his eyes, made him glad he had not been in the Proctors' house any longer.

It had turned into a balmy evening and spring flowers were out in many of the gardens, fresh with the earlier rain. One or two plots in the street had been allowed to revert to nature and sprouted young nettles and straggly grass through which obsolete household goods could be seen. He got into the car, giving the boys a severe look, and drove off. If Ann Proctor had finally decided to tell the truth all they had to do was to inquire at every farmhouse in Norfolk, he thought with disgust. Of course, it would be far simpler than that, he was just worried about Lucy. As long as Maggie Simpson had not married or changed her name during the past three years she would be on the register of electors somewhere, and the job of finding her address would not be his.

Eileen Proctor dressed and put on make-up then went down to tell Sean she was off to bingo with her friends. His response was no more than a grunt as he concentrated on a programme on the television. In his hand was a can of strong lager. At least she would have a few hours of freedom and peace before coming home to face whatever was in store for her. Eileen's problem was that despite the way in which he treated her and even knowing what she did, she still loved him. There was something in him she found strong and masculine and, although she told herself numerous times that she would leave once Ann had married, she knew it would never be.

'Ann, I'm off now,' she called up the stairs as she checked her hair in the hall mirror. 'What time can we expect you back?'

'I'm not sure. Late, I expect,' Ann replied. As usual she would be meeting Richie.

Eileen shut the front door behind her and walked down Culver Road wishing, as she always did, that Sean could make love to her without hitting her first.

'Hi, Lucy, it's me. Moira.'

'Hello. I've been meaning to ring you, but you know what it's like.'

Lucy's voice was flat. Ian had been right, she needed some distraction. He had told her about the pregnancy but she did not know if she ought to mention it. 'Do you fancy lunch? I can take an extra half-hour today.'

'No, I've got some clients to see.' She hesitated then said more positively, 'But why don't we meet after work? Six o'clock in the George?'

'Great, I'll see you there.' It was a place they often used because it was rarely frequented by their husbands or their colleagues. Both of them heard enough shop talk at home.

Moira arrived first and left her jacket and a newspaper proprietorially on one of the comfortable settees against the oak-panelled wall. Two men standing at the bar turned and looked her up and down, taking in her shapely legs beneath the tight-fitting skirt and her soft pale hair. Their encouraging smiles were met with a blank stare. Lucy came in just as Moira was approaching the bar to buy a drink. 'What'll you have?'

'Dry white wine and soda, please.'

Moira said nothing about whether it was wise for her to be drinking, knowing that an occasional glass of something could do more good than harm. Having purchased two glasses of wine they carried them over to the settee, ignoring the two men who were now staring at them openly.

Lucy looked tired and drawn and admitted she was making Barry's life hell. 'I just can't stop worrying that I'm going to lose this baby too.'

It was obviously safe to discuss the subject. 'It's natural, but there's no reason why you should. It was an accident last time, it's not as if there was anything wrong with you or the baby.'

'I know. And I know I'm being unreasonable. I just wish the next fortnight was over with. I've never felt so scared in my life.'

Moira saw it was true and wondered if the real problem was deeper seated. Lucy might not have fully recovered from the depression her loss had caused.

Lucy smiled and her whole face altered. 'Oh, don't look at me like that. I'm not loopy. Fancy some crisps?'

They stayed for a second drink then Moira said she had to go. Both her mother and Mark tended to ring on a Monday night. When she got home there was no sign of Ian or his car. Instead there was a brief message on the answering machine saying not to expect him for supper, he had no idea what time he would be home.

It was the first time Ian had met Enid Mercer and she was younger than he had expected. Her face was unlined and reflected none of the discomfort with which she had to live. The bungalow was neat, with doors wide enough for her chair. 'I have help,' she told him, 'the welfare people are very good.'

Ian smiled. The welfare. It was a dated title, one he had heard often in his youth, but he thought it more appropriate than all the modern departmental names.

The place smelled fresh and the surfaces were clean. Whoever came in took their job seriously. Refusing the offer of tea Ian questioned her about Kelly.

'She came to say goodbye, that much I will say for her, but she refused to say where she was going or why. Dee was equally mysterious. For the life of me I can't think of a reason. She was always such a good child. She didn't stay long and I have to admit I was in some pain at the time so I didn't notice whether she seemed particularly upset herself. I wish I'd taken more notice now.'

'Did she know she stood to inherit?'

'Yes. Not that Dee had a lot to leave, and the house wasn't hers. Mind you, Kelly wasn't mercenary. What really troubles me is why she didn't return for the funeral. She and Dee were close, more like friends really. Mr Roper, do you think something's happened to her?'

'That's what we're trying to find out.' Enid Mercer was not a woman who would be satisfied with platitudes. She had suffered in many ways but she was a survivor. It struck him then that if Kelly had made a point of saying goodbye she had probably left the area of her own accord. There was little more Mrs Mercer could tell him but he stayed and chatted for a while longer. He learned that as a consequence of her husband's death she had been left reasonably well provided for.

'We're not a lucky family,' she stated without irony. 'If Jack hadn't stopped to buy me flowers on his way home from a business trip to London, he would still have been alive. He was killed when a terrorist bomb exploded.'

Mrs Mercer also said she must change her will. She had left everything to Dee and although Kelly was legitimately the next in line she thought it would make things simpler if it was in black and white. 'There's no one else now, only myself and Kelly. Mr Roper, please find her for me.'

'We'll do our best. Now I really must go.'

'Of course. I didn't mean to detain you.' Then, as if it was an afterthought: 'He didn't do it, you know. Owen. He loved her, he would never have harmed her.' She did not expound but there was no need to. The words were spoken with genuine feeling.

To Ian it was a turning point. He was not alone in his conviction even if the other person in question might hold biased views. But Enid Mercer was no fool and had spoken with authoritative certainty.

As Ian made his way back to headquarters he marvelled at her ability to discuss her own future with such equanimity. She had explained the form the progression of her illness

82

would take. 'I wanted Dee to be able to deal with matters when the time came, now it will, God willing, be Kelly. If you don't find her I suppose eventually the hospital or my solicitors will go to court and find me a legal "next friend" to hold power of attorney. I rather like that, don't you? "Next friend", it has a nice ring to it, as if there's someone out there ready to step in to look after you.'

Her comments had helped put his own life in perspective.

Later that day two events occurred almost simultaneously and Ian knew he was in for a long night.

There had been a communication from Norwich to say that a Miss Margaret Simpson had been traced. She lived in a farmhouse in an isolated spot, the only address of which was Fimbrel Cross. What, said the fax, did the Chief Inspector want done about it?

The Chief Inspector, having regained his equilibrium, wanted to have a word or two with Miss Simpson himself. He telephoned Norwich to make sure he would not be treading on anyone's toes and refused to allow the name of the place he was dealing with to remind him of Saturday's disaster. Having ascertained that she was not wanted in connection with a crime, they told him he was free to interview her himself. Tomorrow, with Superintendent Thorne's blessing, he would make another journey. Owen Kerslake, Ian calculated, had been locked up for a little under three weeks. Maybe Ian would soon be certain, one way or the other, whether Owen Kerslake should have been locked up at all. Margaret Simpson had proved to be another elusive character and was surely somehow involved. Ann might not be lying but it appeared that she was being extremely economical with the truth.

'She knows something, I'm sure of it,' Ian muttered as he scrutinised the Simpson woman's address. He had never heard of the place.

He needed to talk to Ann, to use all of his persuasive powers to make her tell him what was on her mind. Margaret Simpson seemed to be the connection between the two girls. That connection could be important.

As he planned how he would approach the Proctors his thoughts were interrupted by the internal telephone. It was another hour before he felt he could leave with a good conscience.

Ann Proctor had said goodbye to her mother as Eileen left for her weekly bingo session and a few minutes later left the house herself. Both her parents believed that she was going to meet Richie as usual. It was not until an evening's television viewing was interrupted by Richie's telephone call that Sean Proctor realised something was seriously wrong. He searched the house on the off-chance that Ann had changed her mind or fallen asleep on her bed then he went down to the bingo hall to consult with his wife. Eileen was strong, she would know what to do. Sean had had enough of the police, he would let her deal with them if necessary.

Eileen passed her sheets of cards over to a neighbour and, tight-lipped with anxiety, returned to Culver Road with Sean.

Richie was waiting on the doorstep. He had already contacted the police, not caring how foolish he might appear. They did not know Ann as he did. She had never let him down and rang even if she was going to be a few minutes late. Something was troubling her, and he wished he had had the sense to force her into telling him what it was. The police had been to see her, that much he did know. It crossed his mind that talking to them might have placed her in danger.

Together they sat and waited, praying that there would not be a second tragedy in Culver Road.

Ian could not believe it. He wanted, more than anything, to be one of the officers calling on the Proctors but it was not a job for a DCI, not at this stage. Ann was free to do as she liked, it was only courtesy which dictated she let her parents or the boyfriend know where she was, yet in his heart he knew her disappearance was connected to the case, just as he knew that the connection between Ann and Kelly was Margaret Simpson.

Before he left, Ian arranged for Ann's employers to be interviewed in the morning if she had not reappeared. Curbing a desire to be everywhere at once, he sighed deeply, switched out the lights in his office and went home.

Ian drew back the bedroom curtains and a wedge of sunlight speckled with dust motes shone across the carpet and his bare feet. The sky was already a deep blue with only a few thin strands of cloud in the distance. They were no bigger than aeroplane vapour trails. It had to be a good omen. Moira flung an arm over her eyes and squinted at him from beneath the bend in her elbow. 'What time is it?'

'Seven o'clock.'

'I didn't hear the alarm.'

'No. I woke before it went off.'

She swung her legs over the side of the bed, tossed back her hair and slipped her arms into an ankle-length dressing-gown. Ian reached out and pulled her to him. She smelled of warmth and sleep and he loved the feel of her flesh through the silky material of her robe. He wished he had more time but he needed to be at the station early.

He envied Moira her ability to get out of bed immediately she woke. It took him several minutes to open his eyes and another ten before he felt ready to move. You were supposed to need less sleep as you got older, he thought, then forced himself not to dwell on the one subject which was, of late, frequently on his mind.

Moira stood on tiptoes and kissed him on the cheek. 'Have you finished in the bathroom?'

'Yes, it's all yours.'

Downstairs he filled the kettle. It could boil while he made his call. Water was gurgling down the outside wash-basin pipe as he dialled the number provided by the Norwich police. Margaret Simpson answered on the third ring.

'Hello.' Her voice was soft but Ian sensed the slightest hesitancy in her tone.

85

Briefly he introduced himself and said that there were one or two matters he'd like to discuss with her but that he would prefer to conduct the interview face to face.

'Must it be here?' she asked.

It was a strange question. Surely she could not be volunteering to drive to Rickenham Green? 'I think it would be better. Will you be at home all day?' Ann Proctor had mentioned the farmhouse, had said something about Miss Simpson having plans for it. It would be interesting to see exactly what they were. A time convenient to them both was arranged and Ian hung up as Moira came downstairs.

'I heard some of that. Will you be home tonight?'

'Yes, but heaven knows what time.' They were in the kitchen. He added cold water to the instant coffee and took a few sips before pouring the rest down the sink. 'No time. I'll ring if I can.' Moira nodded and watched him go.

DS Barry Swan shook his head before Ian had a chance to ask. 'Not a word. The boyfriend's doing his nut. He insists it's completely out of character. Brenda's with the parents now.'

'I'll leave you in charge of it. I'm off to Norfolk.' He left Barry staring after him in surprise.

Despite the new twist Ian found it a pleasure to be driving through the flat, sweeping countryside. Crops were already pushing through the soil, young green shoots which would grow tall and ripen and thus change the whole texture of the landscape.

He left the main road and meandered through lanes which were barely signposted. Delicate clusters of pink and white flowers, the names of which Moira would know, adorned the hedgerows. It was hard to reconcile Dee Mercer's death with this burgeoning fecundity.

The track which led to Fimbrel Cross Farm was uneven but not so badly potholed that Ian need fear for the suspension of the car. At each side of it lay damp mud and he could smell the rich earthiness as his tyres rolled through it. At the end of the lane he had to stop to unhook the latch of a metal barred gate. As he started to push it open a dog began to bark and raced towards him. It stopped several feet away and stood four-square and solid, its canines dangerously sharp beneath drawn-back lips. The coat was a smooth glossy tan. It was not a breed he recognised. When it crouched and gave a throaty growl Ian froze. He was not a natural with animals and had never owned a pet but he had watched with fascination when others spoke in exactly the right tone of voice before walking fearlessly past such an animal. He was speculating as to whether he had time to shut the gate and dive back into the car before the dog sank its fangs into a tender part of his anatomy when a woman's voice called, 'Heel, Caesar.' Ian wondered how the name was spelt. Was it an historical attribution or had he been christened for his behaviour? However, the dog responded and, when directed, retreated into the house. 'It's all right now,' the woman informed him before disappearing herself.

Ian pushed open the gate and drove through, carefully closing it after him. It was his first opportunity to study his surroundings. The building could be nothing other than a farmhouse. It was built of stone, with four windows – two up and two down – equidistant from the door. It was completely plain and there was no garden, only a lawn which had been cut but not weeded.

He parked to one side of the house and walked to the front door which was open. Directly ahead, at the end of a flag-stoned corridor, he saw the outline of the woman through the coloured glass panels in the top half of the back door. The corridor divided the property in half.

The woman came towards him and extended a hand. 'Chief Inspector Roper? I'm Maggie Simpson. Sorry about the delay, I was just shutting the dog up. In here.'

He followed her into a room to his right. The house was quiet and isolated, with an uncarpeted hall and a dog that might have been modelled upon one of the hounds from hell, yet it still exuded peace and warmth. Or perhaps it was Maggie Simpson who did so.

'This is my sitting-room,' she explained as they entered the medium-sized room at the front of the house. The furniture was large, well polished and old, although probably not valuable. It was in keeping with its surroundings as were the chintz curtains and chair covers.

'It's very nice.' And it was, with the sun streaming in through the tall windows which were very clean. But it had been an odd choice of words. Of course it was her sitting-room. He glanced at the two paintings which hung on the walls. They depicted local scenery which he recognised although the artist had lived more than a hundred years ago. Here, he guessed, was a woman who, like himself, resented change for the spurious advantages of progress.

'You've had quite a long drive. I'm sure you're ready for some coffee.'

'I'd love some, thank you.' Her voice was having a soporific effect on him. She would not have found it difficult to control a class of schoolchildren.

'I shan't be long, I've already prepared it.'

He watched her walk from the room. It was a confident walk, her head held high, her narrow shoulders held back. She was short and thin but emanated an inner strength.

Maggie returned with a tray upon which were two earthen-ware mugs, milk, sugar and coffee in a large glass jug with a plunger. She placed the tray on a table between them and before he had a chance to ask why she had chosen to live in such a large house in the middle of nowhere she said, 'I suppose you've been informed of the set-up here.'

He had not been and, curiouser still, Maggie Simpson had at no time queried his reasons for wanting to see her. Ian ad-mitted his ignorance.

'Ah, good, in that case I needn't have worried.'

He had no idea what she was talking about and thought per-haps she had come into money, maybe a great deal of money, and did not want anyone to know about it.

'You see, I'd imagined you'd come about one of the women.'

'The women?'

Maggie gave him a long, shrewd look. 'The women that stay here. Chief Inspector, it seems that you really don't know.'

'Perhaps you'd enlighten me.'

'Will it go any further?'

'Not unless it's necessary.'

'It's a long story, but to summarise, this was my aunt's house, she left it to me. When her husband died she continued farming, and quite successfully too, employing local men. She also took in guests in the summer because she hated to see the rooms empty. Unfortunately I had to sell off a chunk of the land but the rest of the farm is up and running again now.' She paused. 'My aunt brought me up and I've always loved this place and now I've been able to offer to others what my aunt gave to me although it can be harrowing at times. Do you know, I'm getting more and more like her every day but I don't know whether it's because it's in the blood or whether it was her influence.'

Genetics versus environment. Ian thought it was more likely a combination of the two but what he actually said was, 'You think farming is harrowing? Oh, no pun intended.'

'Of course not, that's the easy bit. You have to understand something. I was what is nowadays called the victim of child-abuse. Physical, not sexual. It was years before I would admit it to myself, let alone anyone else. You see, I felt ashamed, as if somehow it was my fault. When my mother married she and my aunt had little contact although I did come and stay once. I suppose she saw the bruises and in-stinctively knew what was happening. I know I didn't tell her. Strange, isn't it, how many people remain loyal to their ab-users?'

Yes, Ian thought and maybe that's what is at the bottom of all this. Three girls, all beautiful – had they been sexually abused?

'I'm sorry, I don't mean to digress but there are certain things you need to know if you're to understand.'

Maggie continued speaking in her soothing voice as Ian studied her. She showed no outward scars of her childhood but she was a level-headed young woman. In faded jeans and a sweatshirt, her feet encased in socks because she had left her boots by the back door and her fine ginger hair pulled back into a pony tail, she seemed totally at ease. She was, Ian de-cided as Maggie folded her feet beneath her on her chair, a woman in whom you could place your trust. She must have been a great teacher and it was easy to see why the girls con-fided in her.

'Even in those days my aunt knew what would happen if

she reported my parents to the relevant authorities; they'd have been on some list or other and I would probably have ended up being taken into care. I've no idea, and I don't suppose my aunt had either, whether she would have been granted custody of me but I doubt it. I hadn't started school then, you see, otherwise someone else might have picked up on what was happening. Anyway, a week after I'd stayed here my aunt arrived unexpectedly at our house. I was told to stay in my room whilst they shut themselves up in the kitchen. God, I was absolutely terrified. I thought I must have done something wrong and my aunt had come to tell my parents. I've no idea what was discussed or how the arrangement came about but the next thing was my mother was packing a suitcase and I was told I was going back to stay at the farm. That was it. I never looked back.'

'And so, Miss Simpson, where is this leading?'

'Call me Maggie, please. To where I am now and to why I assumed you came. This house was my salvation; when I inherited it I decided I wanted it to do the same for others.'

'I see.'

'There are certain agencies who know of our existence but we don't receive any funding – to do so would mean a lack of secrecy. Girls and women come here, those who have suffered abuse, any kind of abuse. It's only a stopping-off point. I suppose we're like a refuge or a hostel but the difference is that no one but the women themselves and me knows where they are. I enforce very strict rules which you may think prejudiced, but from experience I've found I have to. There are no alcoholics or drug-abusers, they are not renowned for keeping their word and, of course, we have no facilities for treatment. And no one is allowed to remain for more than six weeks. They have to sign a pledge of secrecy and before they're accepted we need to know that they are one hundred per cent sure that they are not going to return to whatever they're running away from otherwise the whole thing's a waste of time. So many do, you see – they go back thinking it'll all be different this time.' She shook her head. 'It rarely is once the pattern's been established. This place gives them a breathing space between leaving and finding accommodation and a job. For obvious reasons none of these women are local.'

'So how do they find you?' Ian was genuinely interested.

'Word of mouth.' She smiled and her face lit up. 'You wouldn't believe how many caring people there are out there, people whom we trust and who put these women in touch with us. Several solicitors, for instance.'

'Solicitors?'

'Yes. Think about it, a woman wants a divorce or an injunction taken out against a violent husband, who does she go to? And nine times out of ten a piece of paper doesn't guarantee the brutality will stop. And – ' she looked at him from beneath lowered lashes, 'dare I say it? – the occasional police officer who has dealt with domestic violence. I also have a solicitor friend who gives advice.'

Ian was fascinated. 'So how are you funded?'

'I own the land and the property outright and I invested the money from the piece of land I sold. The overheads aren't great and the women have a choice. If they're in funds they can contribute to their upkeep or they work on the farm for their board. It's mutually beneficial. They retain their pride, the fresh air and exercise are therapeutic, and I don't need to employ outsiders. We manage to turn over a reasonable profit and I think I can safely say that from last year we are now a going concern. I've also had one or two very generous donations. Believe me, these women don't all come from the poorer end of the spectrum.'

Ian was aware of that fact. However, he decided it was time to get on to the purpose of his visit. 'Maggie . . . ' But before he could continue she had raised a hand in warning.

'Whatever it is you've come for I'd like you to promise me one thing, that you won't divulge what I've told you to anyone.'

'You have my word.' He paused. 'Unless I feel you're needed.'

She smiled again in acknowledgement of what he was saying. 'Thank you. You're very kind. I didn't expect to make another contact out of your visit.'

'So this is the reason you left Rickenham Comprehensive so suddenly?'

'Did Jean Adams say that? It wasn't that sudden. I gave plenty of notice. I think it was more unexpected. I decided to stay on at the school until some necessary repairs were done and the probate was sorted out. You see, I was still unsure how to put the house to good use. Then one of the girls came to me with a problem, one she felt unable to discuss with her year tutor, and I immediately knew what I had to do. At first I'd thought I'd like to help people educationally but that clinched it.'

'And would that girl's name be Kelly Mercer by any chance?' Ian watched the colour drain from her face. There was no need for an answer.

'How did you know that?'

'I didn't. You must have read of her mother's murder.'

'Yes.'

'So presumably you know that we're still looking for Kelly.'

'Looking for her?'

'Are you saying you didn't know that she was missing, that she didn't turn up for the funeral?'

'Oh, God, no. No, I didn't know that.'

'Do you know where she is?'

'I couldn't tell you if I did. If it got out that I was passing on information like that to the police no one would want to come here.'

'I take your point, but what if she's in danger? Or dead?'

Maggie Simpson straightened her legs and poured out the remains of the coffee. Her face was serious as she questioned her conscience.

'Kelly was here, about two and a half years ago. After she confided in me I knew she would be leaving at the end of the year. Sensibly she stayed on to take her exams. I spent an hour talking to her, trying to persuade her that she should do her A levels, at another school or college maybe, but I think she'd lost heart. I told her I was leaving at the end of that term but if she stuck it out until after her GCSEs there would be a place for her here. She was my first one. She arrived about two weeks into the summer holidays. When she didn't come at once I hoped she'd resolved her problems and was going to go back to school but I think she used the time to make certain

92

she knew what she was doing. She stayed for four or five weeks.'

'And after that?'

'I can't tell you.'

'Maggie – '

'No. I said I can't, not won't. She left as suddenly as she arrived and I didn't even know if she'd got any money.'

Ian sighed. He had come so far, physically as well as mentally, only to reach a dead end. 'You couldn't hazard a guess? Wasn't there anything she said which might have given you a clue?'

'Not that I can remember – it's a long time ago now. Although I do recall that she once said she'd never been to London. Of course, that doesn't mean it was where she was heading.'

London. It made sense. It was where so many runaways made for but it would be like looking for a needle in a haystack and she would probably be calling herself something else. 'You haven't heard from her since?'

'Not a word.' Maggie was frowning. 'I'm sorry, but there's something else, I just can't think what it is.' Ian waited. 'Yes, she said she'd like to work with children. It would have suited her, she had endless patience.'

'Her problem, Maggie – was it the man who moved in with her mother, Owen Kerslake?'

She shook her head vehemently. The pony tail swung widely. 'From what she told me Owen was a father to her. There were no complications there. Oh, God, I suppose you'll have to know. She was being blackmailed.'

'By whom?'

'That's what she wouldn't tell me and I knew there was more to it than that. There was something seriously troubling the girl. Of course, young people sometimes worry needlessly but I don't think so in Kelly's case.' Her green eyes widened. 'You don't think her mother's death has anything to do with her?'

'That's what we're trying to find out.'

'But I thought you'd arrested someone.'

'We have. But we still feel that Kelly holds the key to it all.'

'Can I ask what led you to me?'

'We were following up everyone who had had contact with Kelly prior to her leaving, especially members of staff who left around the same time.'

'Then you'll have spoken to Derek Cavanagh. Don't look so surprised, Kelly told me he was going at the end of the year. Poor sod. His wife was having an affair with John Fletcher, everyone knew about it except Derek. I suppose he decided to leave when he found out.'

Thank you, Ian thought. It was confirmation of Cavanagh's story although it did not prove that he had not taken the photograph of Kelly. But Cavanagh a blackmailer? He could not see it. 'I think I've taken up enough of your time. Thank you for the coffee.'

'My pleasure. Would you like to look around the place before you go?'

Ian glanced at his watch. There was the matter of Ann Proctor awaiting him but his team were perfectly capable of dealing with it. 'Yes, I'd like that.'

'I need some privacy and I also need to keep some distance from the women, it's better they socialise together, hence my sitting-room.' They went out into the corridor and Ian was shown the communal kitchen and living area but, quite rightly, not the bedrooms.

In the bright sunshine he listened to Maggie Simpson talk knowledgeably and enthusiastically about her project. In the distance he saw some women at work but Maggie made no move to introduce him to them. 'By the way, what can you tell me about Ann Proctor?'

'Ann? Nothing really. She was a quiet girl, well behaved. She worked hard but she wasn't quite up to qualifying for further education if I recall. At least, not when she was in my year.'

'But she talked to you?'

'Who, Ann? I don't think so.'

Ian stopped walking and turned to look at her. 'Are you sure?'

'Well, of course she talked to me, but only about school-work, and not much once she left my year.'

'Then tell me, Maggie, how did she know about the farm?'

Maggie swung around, open-mouthed. 'But she can't do.'

94

She paused. 'Unless . . . ' But there was no need to continue. They were both thinking the same thing. Unless Kelly had told her.

8

DC Alan Campbell, pedant that he was, had meticulously prepared the Kerslake file for the DPP. Statements, witness statements, forensic reports and the results of the post-mortem were clipped together in chronological order. Because he was so meticulous and because his main pleasure in life came from marrying up facts and figures, something had stuck in his mind. During his lunch break he went to find the police copy of the file.

He had never been able to understand what his colleagues referred to as a 'feel' for something, a sense that something was wrong or someone was lying. He liked to base things on hard facts. Since his divorce he had become even more pernickety but no one was sure whether this was to compensate for what he thought of as his biggest mistake or whether his wife had been responsible for making sure this trait did not become out of hand but was no longer there to curb it.

The Chief now, he thought as he flicked through the file, he believes Kerslake is innocent. He obviously had a 'feel' for it. On the other hand, the Chief was three rungs further up the ladder than he was and had got there by realising that although your senses could often be more wrong than right they should not be ignored. Hence the reason Alan Campbell was destined to remain at his present rank. He *liked* doing jobs that the others detested, he enjoyed checking and double-checking, he preferred playing around with the facts to hand rather than going out seeking new ones.

Then why, he thought, am I wasting a precious half-hour of free time reading this?

He had not been in attendance at the post-mortem but re-called that the pathologist's examination had shown that Dee had last eaten about twelve hours before her death. The latest sighting of her was at nine forty-five in the morning when she was returning from the local shop which was half a mile away. Kerslake had told them that she was not due to start work until six that evening and this was borne out by Charlie Braithwaite, the owner of the chip shop. Braithwaite had last seen Dee the previous night when she had left just after ten with some haddock and chips which would otherwise have been thrown away. Only on Fridays and Saturdays did he stay open until eleven.

Campbell realised what was bothering him but assumed he must be wrong because someone else would have picked it up.

The Last Supper was how he thought of it. When he and his family had moved from the Highlands to Glasgow he was sent down the road for the monthly treat of three fish suppers for the family. It was certainly Dee's last fish supper. This was as close to a joke as Campbell was capable of making.

Alan Campbell was stick insect thin but forever hungry. What he found hard to understand was how Dee had managed to survive from ten thirty when she reached home after work that night with the haddock until at least one ten, one fifteen the following lunchtime which was the earliest that Kerslake could have got back from working on the house he was painting. Impossible that he had killed her before he left for work. His alibi was watertight and Dee had been seen by a neighbour. Not even a biscuit, he thought. She had been preparing a meal at the time she was killed which, to Alan's mind, suggested it was more likely to be mid-morning as a slow-cooker had been warming. He was no expert on domestic arrangements but he thought lunchtime or later would not give the meat long enough to cook. It would also be more sensible to get the chores out of the way before taking a lunch-time break.

He had, though, heard female officers discussing diets in the canteen and knew that some of them could go all day without eating. Perhaps Dee was such a woman, especially if she worked with food, it might have dulled her appetite. As a reminder his own stomach growled. He put the file back and went down to the canteen and demolished a meat pie, mashed potato and peas and a doughnut with his cup of tea.

Judy Robbins, in her tight-fitting uniform, watched him with amazement thinking how unfair life was. Hers was a constant struggle to remain a size 16. She took a few more mouthfuls of the rather limp salad and wondered why DC Campbell was grinning inanely to himself. She did not know that he believed he had, for the first time, experienced that gut feeling and that he was about to do something unheard of as far as he was concerned. He was going to act on his own initiative.

Maggie Simpson spent the rest of the day thinking about Kelly and what might have happened to her. With her looks, if she had gone to London, she might have landed in all sorts of trouble. She did not know the whole story but she thought that Lizzie Conrad and Michelle Short might have been mixed up in it too. It was a pity she hadn't been able to persuade Kelly to confide in her further.

There were four women with her at the moment, two of them married, one a sixteen-year-old girl whose father beat her with a belt and who was still recovering from her injuries. She had refused to press charges when the police were called to the hospital and, terrified that they might act without her permission and more terrified of what might await her when she went home, she had discharged herself. A doctor at the hospital had been waiting for her downstairs and told her about Fimbrel Cross Farm. The fourth girl, aged about twenty, had arrived two days ago and, so far, had hardly said a word. It was an unspoken agreement that nothing was forced, the women would open up when they were ready to.

With her mind half on Kelly and half on the new girl, whose name was Joanna, she was not expecting a knock on the door. It was five fifteen. Joanna was in the kitchen preparing a meal and the other three were working outside. Maggie put down the agricultural catalogue which she was supposed to be studying and went to open the door telling

Caesar, who had already started barking, to stay where he was.

For several seconds Maggie did not believe what she was seeing. 'Ann?'

Ann Proctor nodded. Her lips quivered then she burst into tears. Maggie put an arm around her shoulders and led her inside.

DC Campbell was to join Markham on another project that afternoon and he was treated to his colleague's usual brand of charm. 'Stop dreaming, Campbell, and let's get this sodding case sorted.' They worked in virtual silence for an hour or so until they needed to converse on what they had found. After a few telephone calls Markham seemed happier and said he was calling it a day. 'Going for a pint?'

'I might later.'

'Please yourself.' And with that Markham was gone.

The Chief was nowhere to be found so Alan informed DS Swan of his intentions although he seemed not to be listening. He shrugged and went out to his car then headed in the direction of Braithwaite's fish and chip shop, The In Plaice as it was whimsically named.

It was only a few minutes after six and he did not think it would be busy yet. Having parked in the next street where there were no restrictions, he rounded the corner and was assailed by wafts of frying food. The acid in his stomach responded and he realised he was hungry again. Whatever came of the interview he wouldn't leave without something to eat.

Braithwaite was shovelling the first batch of chips out of the fryer to drain before they went into the heated cabinet. Several pieces of fish, some battered sausages and chicken pies were already on display. There were pickled eggs and pickled onions in huge jars on the counter. Campbell eyed them all longingly.

It was hot in the elongated, narrow premises. The counter was at the front, at right angles to the door, and further back were several tables set against one side of the wall. 'Mr Braithwaite?'

'Police.' It was not a question. He carried on scooping out chips then tipped a large bag of sliced potatoes into the deep fryer. The golden fat bubbled and gurgled. Braithwaite pulled down the cylindrical lid.

Alan smiled, unusual in that he was flattered to be spotted for what he was. 'Yes. I wonder if I might ask you a few more questions.'

'About Dee? I still can't get over it. She was such an asset here. She had such a way with the customers, she could always raise a smile. That's important in this business with all the competition we've got these days from the other takeaways. Go on, fire away.'

'Firstly, did she talk much about her daughter?'

'Young Kelly? Not a lot. She used to bring her in when she was small but I suppose later, like a lot of young girls, she was watching her figure. They don't know what they're missing.'

Alan agreed wholeheartedly with that statement. 'But did she mention her recently, like where she was?'

'No.' Braithwaite rubbed his chin. 'A bit of a mystery now I think about it. She told me she was moving away but she never said where. Still, she said she was doing well.'

'In what way?'

'I dunno. Just that she was getting on all right.'

It could be that Dee had said it to make things sound normal, but Alan hoped it was because she had actually been in touch with her.

'I'm glad you got the bastard. I keep thinking about it, I can't believe it's happened, and to Dee, of all people. It just goes to show, you can't tell, can you? She seemed so happy and it was Owen this and Owen that.' He wiped his brow with a clean white handkerchief which he took from the pocket of his white coat.

'This is going to sound like a peculiar question, but did she have a good appetite?'

'She enjoyed my fish and chips all right. They're good, mind, although I say it myself. I don't know really.' He considered the question for a second or two. 'She wasn't exactly small, was she? Not fat, like, but well built. She'd tell me what

99

she was cooking sometimes, we talked about food a lot, we two, and she never refused anything that was left over. Just a minute.' A customer had entered the shop. Campbell hoped he did not want to sit down to eat. He was immediately followed by two small boys who were counting their money and debating how much they could get with what they possessed.

Alan stepped out of the way and tried to appear inconspicuous. Within a few minutes the shop was empty again.

'So she wasn't on a diet or anything?'

'No, not Dee.'

'Would she have eaten something before she came to work, like just before or maybe at dinnertime?'

'You're right, you are, real peculiar questions. I suppose so, it'd be too long to go until after she finished, especially if she was working a weekend.'

Alan Campbell wasn't sure if he had gained anything or not but he would report his visit to the Chief and explain his theory. 'Well, that's all I wanted to know. Thanks. Now, I'll have a fish supper to take out.'

'A fish supper. Haven't heard that expression for ages. Cod or haddock?'

'Haddock, please.'

Braithwaite deftly slid the food into an oblong waxed container and wrapped it in sheets of white paper, regretting the disappearance of the days when he used newspaper. It tasted better somehow. 'That's all right, take it, it's on the house.'

'No, please, I couldn't.' Alan was fumbling for change.

Braithwaite tipped back his head and let out a bellow of laughter. The young officer was scarlet with embarrassment. 'Go on, take it. I can't imagine even the Chief Constable interpreting a fish supper as a bribe or protection money.'

Alan, seeing that he was not going to be allowed to pay, hurried off the premises. His puritanical upbringing told him that he should have left the money on the counter anyway. He sat behind the wheel of the car and ate the fish and chips, his enjoyment spoiled by his guilt.

100

*

Barry Swan swung a chair around and sat astride it, his arms resting along its back as he faced the Chief. 'I've run rings round the boy but he's adamant he doesn't know why she's taken it into her head to disappear. He's worried sick, so are her parents.' Richie Howlett had taken the day off work and Barry had gone to see him in his bedsit.

'It's just not like her, she's never done anything like this before and ever since the . . . ever since what's happened, she's been very nervous,' Richie had said, gripping his hands together convulsively due to the state of his own mind. He had not been able to suggest anywhere Ann might have gone.

'I don't like it. Have you ever known a case where the main players are made out to be so pure but at the same time appear to be hiding things not only from us but from each other?' Ian sighed in exasperation.

'I agree. It's the same all over again with this girl. According to Brenda, Eileen Proctor stressed what a good daughter Ann is. She's convinced she wouldn't take it into her head to do a bunk and that something's happened to her. Another one who, so they'd have us believe, was cast in the angelic mould.'

'Yes. But we've got an absence of angels now. Where is Brenda, by the way?' Ian did not notice the mental connection his brain had subconsciously made.

'She was talking to Campbell a few minutes ago. If you want to see her she'll be up soon. She said she was on her way.'

'Good.' Ian stood and wandered over to the window. Hands clasped behind his back he gazed down into the street. Finding nothing there to inspire him he lit a cigarette and blew a plume of smoke against the already smeared glass. Barry lit one of his own. He had cut down during Lucy's pregnancy but had not been able to give up completely.

There was a quick tap on the door and DC Gibbons appeared. Dressed in loosely cut trousers and a soft blouse she was both elegant and sensuous. 'I didn't get anywhere with the parents, sir.'

'So Sergeant Swan told me.'

'The mother just kept crying and thinking the worst. The

101

father's altogether different. Not only is he suspicious of us, he's angry that Ann's put the family in the position where we need to be involved. They've contacted all their family and friends, especially Ann's; not that she's got many, she spends most of her time with Richie Howlett. No one's heard from her. It's just like Kelly all over again except this time not even her mother knows where she is.'

'If Kelly's mother ever did. Have we checked the Proctors' CV?'

'Yes, sir. They're both clean. Constable Campbell did it.'

Yes, Ian thought, Campbell would have done. He had also come up with a strange but interesting theory about Dee Mercer's eating habits which might or might not mean anything but at least showed Campbell was capable of thinking for himself. Campbell was probably right. There was never an exact time of death and even the most careful of pathological investigations could only produce an estimate. 'Look, we seem to be chasing our tails here. I think, for the moment, we'd better forget Kerslake and concentrate on these girls. If there's a connection we need to find it and if there isn't, well, God help us all. Let's go back to square one. Brenda, you go and have a little chat with Lizzie Conrad. She'll at least have known Ann as they were in the same class. I'm not sure yet what to do about the Short girl, but if she was as close to Conrad and Kelly Mercer as people say then they *must* have exchanged some confidences. Come on, I've had a gutful, let's leave it at that for today.'

Brenda made her excuses, she was not spending the evening going over old ground in the pub. In the ladies' toilets she loosened her hair, sprayed on perfume and donned a jacket which matched her trousers. The lipstick she applied seemed a little garish. She rubbed some off and applied lip gloss. She was meeting Andrew Osborne and was not sure how she felt about it. It was, she supposed, the first real date she had had since she had sent Harry packing. At least she and Andrew were starting on an equal footing, both were divorced and neither had children to complicate matters. Starting? She stared at her reflection in the long mirror which ran the length of the basins. It was far too soon to be thinking long term. But

102

Andrew was intelligent and humorous and she liked his off-beat looks.

Unaware that she was under discussion, she left the building and made her way to the George where she was unlikely to meet anyone from work.

'She's very cheerful lately,' Barry commented several minutes later.

'Who? Brenda? Yes, but she's never gloomy like some I could name.' Ian stroked his chin. He had a strong suspicion it was to do with that solicitor but kept the thought to himself. He did not gossip and did not encourage it in others. 'Look, why don't you give Lucy a ring and see if she feels like coming out? I'm meeting Moira at eight. We thought we'd try that new Greek place, the one that used to be that greasy spoon. It'll make a change, every new restaurant these days seems to be Indian.'

'I should've thought you'd be delighted,' Barry replied as he reached for the telephone and dialled his home number.

Lucy agreed to join them; Barry was pleased that her response was immediate and that her tone was not as flat and dull as it had been. She had not been sick for the previous three mornings, which probably had a lot to do with it.

Ian had an hour to kill but knew it would be unwise to spend it in the pub where he would get a head start on the others. Instead he spent the time scribbling names on a bit of paper and as he did so he became more and more convinced that what he had felt in Maggie Simpson's company was more than a hunch. He decided he wanted to know what Michelle Short looked like. Was she as good-looking as the other girls, and, if so, what relevance did it have? His brain was racing, a result of thinking too hard. He knew it was better to have a few hours off, to relax; that was when ideas and comprehension often occurred. Child abuse? If so then Ann Proctor had nothing to fear, not if Kerslake had been responsible. Yet Ian couldn't see Owen Kerslake in that role and Ann hadn't been part of Kelly's set. She knew something, though, of that he was certain.

Maggie Simpson introduced Ann to the other women, but only used their first names. She knew the priorities and ensured Ann ate a proper meal before she allowed her to talk. There was still the problem of where she was to sleep. There were four bedrooms and already two of the women were sharing but Maggie did not possess another bed. She made a mental note to purchase one which she could fold up and store somewhere if such a contingency arose again. She did not wish to have to turn people away and it was for that reason that there was a time limit on the duration of their stay.

In her own sitting-room she gently questioned Ann. 'You know whatever you say will go no further. Do you want to tell me why you've left home?'

'I can't.'

'Are you hurt in any way?'

Ann shook her head. 'No. No one's touched me. That's not why I came.'

Maggie chewed the inside of her cheek. If the girl had not been abused she ought not to be there, but something was troubling Ann. She was shaking from head to foot and there was genuine fear in her eyes. Fear and something else, although Maggie could not decipher what it was. 'Does anyone know where you are?'

'No.' A faint flush appeared in her cheeks. 'They'll be worried sick by now.'

'When did you leave Rickenham Green?'

'Yesterday. I hitched lifts. I got bed and breakfast last night because I wasn't sure if I'd be welcome here. It isn't as if – '

'It's all right,' Maggie interrupted. 'Everyone's welcome. Ann, you do realise your parents might have called the police?'

'I know, but I don't suppose they'll do much. I'm over eighteen and I'm not in any trouble.' She paused. 'Not as far as the police are concerned. I just couldn't face it, all those questions about Kelly and her mother. I knew if I stayed I'd . . .' but she did not finish the sentence.

Maggie had already worked out that there had to be a connection between Ann's arrival and Kelly Mercer, especially as the Chief Inspector had mentioned both names. 'Did Kelly tell you about this place?'

'Yes. And she made me swear I wouldn't tell anyone else, not unless I thought they needed to come here.'

'Why do you think she told you?'

'She said I might need your help at some point.'

'Why should she think that?'

'I don't know.' Ann did know and it was a secret she would have to keep for ever. Even from Richie. Oh, Richie, she thought, he'll be going mad with worry. Tears sprang into her eyes as she thought of him. Maybe they could forget the big white wedding and get married right away, just the two of them and witnesses in a register office. Her parents would be disappointed but it might provide the solution and she would no longer be living at home.

'Ann, when did Kelly tell you about Fimbrel Cross Farm?'

'Recently.'

Maggie was startled. Obviously the police didn't know that or she would not have received a visit from them. 'Recently? Then she's safe?'

'Yes. She's in London, training as a children's nurse.'

'Thank goodness for that.' Maggie had feared that she might have found a less salubrious method of earning a living, especially after what she had been subjected to. 'And she's happy?'

'Very. She said she loves the work and is pleased now that she didn't go back to school. She's living in hospital accommodation.'

'Did her mother know this?' It would have been hard on Dee Mercer to die without being aware that her daughter was both safe and happy.

'Of course. They kept in touch by telephone.'

Relieved, Maggie said she would make them some coffee. When she returned bearing two mugs she asked the question which had puzzled her most. 'If what you've said is true, then why didn't Kelly go home for the funeral?'

'Because she was scared. She asked me to put some flowers on the grave after it was over.'

For some unknown reason Maggie suddenly remembered her aunt's sun lounger which was stored in the shed and wondered whether it would be more comfortable than the floor to

105

sleep on. At least she had plenty of bedding. As they talked she had come to a decision. Ann could stay the one night but in the morning she would have to make other arrangements. It was not fair to anyone who might need her services more urgently and Ann had a choice of places at which to stay. Besides, she was part of a police inquiry and Maggie was in the unfortunate position of struggling with her conscience. She ought, by rights, to let the police or Ann's family know where she was. Under other circumstances – if Ann had been injured or abused in any other way – she would not have considered such a move, but this was different. She had never yet breached a confidence but she was sure the police were searching for the girl and she, herself, might be breaking the law. If that were the case she might lose all that she had gained, and how much worse that would be for the women she sheltered.

Ann was to sleep in the communal sitting-room. Maggie had no intention of offering her her own bed and it would be a mistake to allow her to become too comfortable. At eleven she left Ann to it and went upstairs to bed where she tossed and turned throughout the night.

She was the first up and woke Ann at seven fifteen with a cup of tea. 'There's sugar if you want it. Okay. Look, I need to talk to you. I know it's early and I know you've got problems but I can't keep you here. For a start I haven't the room.' Maggie grabbed a high-backed chair from around the dining-table and sat down. 'I'm sorry, love, but I really think we ought to let someone know where you are. Your parents – '

'No.' The retort was vehement. 'No, not them,' she continued more quietly.

'Who then?'

'Richie. My boyfriend. He'll come and get me. I can stay with him.'

And, Maggie thought, as soon as she rings him he'll tell the police which leaves me in somewhat of a predicament. 'This is a sanctuary, Ann, the fewer people who know about it, the better. There's a man I know who is completely trustworthy. Will you let me tell him instead?'

106

'Who is it?' Ann brushed her long hair out of her eyes. Still tired, she looked very young and vulnerable.

'He's called – well, he's a policeman actually.' She stopped just in time. Chief Inspector Roper might well have been one of the officers who had already spoken to Ann. 'He's been here, he knows about us and he won't let on where you've been.'

Ann was too upset to have noticed the omission of the man's name. 'All right,' she agreed with a sigh. 'I know I can't stay here indefinitely anyway. But can I let Richie know as well?'

'Yes. Once I've made my call.'

The Greek meal had been a success but the party had disbanded relatively early because Lucy found she tired quickly. Consequently Ian was up at seven forty when the telephone rang. DC Brenda Gibbons apologised for ringing him at home but said she thought he'd want to know.

'You're in early. Anyway, know what?'

Brenda did not say that she had had a restless night because she had been thinking about Andrew Osborne and where their relationship might lead. They had gone to the cinema then had a meal and he had seen her safely to her door then left without touching her. 'Maggie Simpson's been on the phone. She wants to speak to you urgently. Only you, she's refused to discuss whatever it is with anyone else.'

'Give me her number and I'll call her from here.' Brenda recited it and Ian wrote it on the pad beside the phone. 'Depending on what she says you'd better let them know to expect me when they see me at the station.' Ian hung up. Because he always had a wet shave and his face had been half covered with foam when the call came, there were blobs of it on the receiver and the pen with which he had written down the number was sticky.

Maggie must have been waiting for the call because she answered on the first ring. 'Thank you for getting back to me so quickly. Look, I knew I had to tell someone and you were

107

the only one I could think of. I suppose you know Ann Proctor left home?'

'Yes.'

'She's here, with me. She's all right, no injuries or anything, but in a bit of a state emotionally. I know I should have reported – '

'It's all right. I understand. The main thing is that she's safe.' Relief prevented him from chiding Maggie for not having reported it immediately. And he did understand her dilemma. If Ann's whereabouts had become public knowledge, or word had got out that it was a place to hide, then Fimbrel Cross Farm would no longer be able to serve its purpose. 'Has she spoken to you?'

'Not exactly. She's got problems and I get the feeling they're to do with her parents, although Kelly seems to be mixed up in it too.'

'Kelly Mercer?'

'Yes. But I think it'd be better if you heard it from Ann.'

'I can come and fetch her.'

'I don't think she'll agree to that, although I did explain that I was not going to allow anyone other than you to collect her from here. She wants Richie Howlett to come for her but it's on the understanding that I drop her into Norwich and he meets her there. I'll stay with her until he arrives.'

'That's fine by me. As long as the lad doesn't decide they might as well head for Gretna Green or something.' But Ian did not think he would – and Richie's going up there would save police resources.

'I'll tell her. She's shaken and worried but deep down she wants to go back.'

'Fine. Oh, and, Maggie, I'll make sure there're no repercussions your end.'

'God bless you,' she said quietly, replacing the receiver before Ian had a chance to say anything more.

'Don't the criminal fraternity ever sleep?' Moira asked rather waspishly as she came down the stairs in her dressing-gown. 'I'm owed an hour, I don't need to be in until ten.'

'Sod's law. The phone always goes when you want a lie-in.'

'You're looking smug. What's happened?'

108

'The girl's turned up.'

'Kelly Mercer?'

'No. The other one, but it seems she might know more about Kelly than she's been letting on.' Ian paused. 'Well, as you *are* up and as you don't have to be in for ages yet, how about making your old man a proper breakfast?'

The look she gave him before she went back upstairs suggested he might as well drop dead. Ian shrugged and, smiling optimistically, went to fill the coffee machine. It would not be until quite late in the afternoon that he would be able to interview Ann Proctor. Richie Howlett needed time to get to Norwich and back again and he might well take a break for something to eat and a chance to speak to his fiancée before they got back. By that time DC Gibbons would also have had a heart-to-heart with Lizzie Conrad. He wondered now if it might not have been wiser to send a female in the first place.

Lizzie had been offered staff accommodation at the hotel but had opted for her own bedsit. She knew from conversations that there was little privacy amongst those who chose to stay at the Duke of Clarence. They were in and out of each other's rooms which were, besides, cramped and too hot in the summer because they were the old servants' quarters under the eaves. Financially she was no worse off because her salary was not liable for the reduction for bed and board.

Her shift that day was from two until ten and she had planned to spend the morning shopping for food and buying something to wear for the weekend, which she had off. On Saturday she was going to a club with a couple of girlfriends. She frowned when DC Gibbons knocked on the door and introduced herself. She hoped it would not take long.

Brenda had gained access by pressing the buzzer next to the name Conrad on the entry-phone, thinking how sensible the girl was not to advertise the fact that she was female. The address was Saxborough Road where almost every property had been converted into flats or bedsits, and it would have been easy to deduce that Lizzie lived there alone. Many teenagers moved into the area as the first step towards becoming independent. Brenda had lived somewhere similar herself once. Number 8 was a little less dilapidated than most, and window boxes trailed dusty ivy and some brown-headed daffodils which the occupants had not got around to replacing.

'You'd better come in then,' Lizzie said when Brenda had reached the first floor. The girl had been waiting in the open doorway.

Brenda stepped straight into the main living area. The room was large and high-ceilinged with a picture rail and ornate stucco moulding around the central light fitting. Once it must have been impressive. Now the carpet was faded and threadbare, the furniture cheap and none too soild.

In one corner was a single divan over which was thrown a patchwork quilt and some scatter cushions which did nothing to disguise the function of the bed. There was a door leading to what seemed to be a cupboard built into another corner but which held a shower unit, wash-basin and toilet. The kitchen was hidden behind a curtain.

'Would you like some coffee?' Lizzie wanted some herself and saw no reason why she should be deprived of it because she had a visitor.

'Please.'

'It's only instant.'

'That's fine.' Brenda wondered why people always made excuses for not providing coffee they had ground and percolated themselves. To her mind it was a waste of time and, anyway, she preferred instant.

Without being invited to, Brenda sat at one of the three chairs around a small deal table in the window. The net curtain, she noticed, was very white.

'An inspector came to see me at work the other day. Is this about the same thing? Kelly Mercer?'

'Chief Inspector. And yes, it is.' Brenda spooned sugar into her mug. 'We think she ran away because something was seriously troubling her. We also think you may know what it was.'

110

Lizzie did not look up when she said, 'Kelly didn't confide in me.'

'Wasn't that strange considering, on your own admission, you were such close friends?'

'She may have said something to Michelle.'

'We've already spoken to Michelle.' There was no elaboration on the statement.

'Oh, have you?' Lizzie Conrad was stirring her coffee, watching the liquid swirl in the mug. She could not resist asking, 'What did she say?'

'I'm not at liberty to tell you that.' The Chief was right, she thought, all the girls were exceptionally good-looking. Even in jeans and a sweatshirt Lizzie Conrad was stunning.

'Can I ask if she mentioned me at all?'

'Why should she?'

Lizzie shrugged. 'I don't know. I was just curious. You see, we don't keep in touch as often as we intended. At first we wrote but you know how it is, when one of you goes away things change. Well, I suppose I mean that people change. I saw Michelle a couple of times during the Christmas vacation but we haven't written to each other since.'

Brenda recognised that the inconsequential details were a way of diverting her from the subject under discussion. 'We believe that Kelly was involved in something she preferred to keep a secret. We also believe that she wasn't the only one. Add to this Ann Proctor's disappearance and you can see why we're so concerned. It all seems to revolve around girls who were in the same class at school.'

'Ann? Never.' Lizzie was startled. She had not meant to blurt the words out.

'What's puzzling you, Miss Conrad?'

'I was just surprised that she's run off, that's all. I didn't mean . . .' She stopped.

Brenda nodded and mentally finished the sentence for her. I didn't mean she wasn't the sort of girl to become involved with the rest of us. But involved in what? 'So you know nothing about Ann, where she might be, for instance, or her reasons for disappearing?'

A closed expression came over the girl's face before she

111

smiled and looked Brenda straight in the eye. 'I've no idea where she is. To be honest, I haven't spoken to her for ages and I certainly can't think of any reason why she'd up and off. Oh, and in case you decide to check up on me, I've noticed her behind the till in Fine Fare occasionally but she's always too busy to speak.'

To Brenda the signs were obvious. There was nothing to be gained by staying because Lizzie Conrad had decided she had nothing more to say. Brenda played her last card. 'You've no plans for leaving Rickenham Green yourself, have you?'

'Good heavens, none. Why?'

'Because it may be necessary for us to speak to you again. And do be careful, make sure you lock your doors at night.' Brenda hooked the strap of her bag over her shoulder and stood up, suppressing a smile. Lizzie Conrad was worried, that much was obvious, but Brenda had the feeling that it was to do with the past rather than with present events. She had rattled the girl, but was it enough to make her talk? What had they done? The natural conclusion had to be something to do with drugs or sex. Brenda chided herself. She was becoming as lewd as the men. 'Okay, thank you for the coffee. I'll see myself out.'

Brenda returned to the station disappointed that her efforts had produced no more than the Chief's. 'Has the Short girl been seen again?' she asked DS Swan who was in the corridor with a file under his arm and a polystyrene container of coffee in his hand.

'Not yet. The Chief said to wait and see what you came up with first.'

'Sweet FA. Lizzie Conrad's hiding something, though, and she wanted to know what Michelle had said about her. I'm damn sure that whatever was or is going on, the three of them were in it together. What I can't see is where Ann Proctor fits in.'

'Hopefully we'll know later today. She and Richie Howlett are on their way back. He rang from a pay-phone in Norwich to let us know he'd picked her up safely. He also said she's scared but she won't talk to him.'

'I suspected that boy would keep to his word. Let's hope

she's scared enough to talk to us. I've been meaning to ask, how's Lucy?' Like everyone else at headquarters she knew about the miscarriage. Despite Barry only having told Ian his wife was pregnant the word had got around. PC Judy Robbins had known, of course, as she was Lucy's best friend, but she had not said anything. But one of the uniformed officers was going out with a nurse from Rickenham General where Lucy had been admitted and had probably been the source of the information.

'She's fine.' Barry paused. 'Actually, she's pregnant again.'

'That's marvellous. Congratulations.'

'We're not celebrating yet. We want to get through the next ten days before we start relaxing.'

'I can understand that. Look, I won't say anything.' Brenda flung back her hair as she began to walk away.

'Wait.' Barry looked embarrassed. He had spoken too loudly and drawn the attention of other people passing. 'Wait,' he repeated more softly. 'I think it might be better if it was common knowledge. We kept it quiet last time and look what happened. You can spread the word, that's fine by me.'

Brenda considered what he said. 'No. It'll seem too much like gossip, Barry. I think it would be better coming from you.'

He nodded. 'You're right. Anyway, if the subject crops up it's okay to say something.'

Brenda walked away leaving Barry staring after her. How different he was from the rumours she had heard about him before her days at Rickenham. Vain, arrogant, boastful, womanising – these were just a few of the adjectives which had been linked to his name. She did not know that meeting Lucy had altered him almost overnight and that he had suddenly grown up.

'Yes,' Barry muttered, trying to remember what he was supposed to be doing with the file he was carrying. 'It is up to me.'

'What is?' Markham glared at him. Barry was blocking the way and Markham was laden with a large cardboard box containing recovered stolen goods which he was delivering to the exhibits officer on the case.

'Telling people that my wife's having a baby.'

113

Markham surprised him with one of his rare grins. 'Still got some lead in it, then?' was his congratulatory phrase before pushing past and continuing on his way.

Almost a show of emotion, Barry thought, as he remembered where he was supposed to be going. The file contained information regarding the burglaries in the area which suddenly seemed to have abated. He took it to the general office where DC Campbell awaited it.

'I suspect they're heading south,' Campbell guessed. 'They're organised and they're not youths. Silver, gold and small antiques is all they take. The last place they did contained more electronic devices than Dixon's but they didn't touch them.'

'I think you're right.' Barry's mind went back over what Campbell had suggested to the Chief about the time Dee Mercer last ate. The man was now expressing another opinion. Wonders would never cease. He did not want to stay and chat; like Ian, his mind was on the latter part of the day and what Ann Proctor might have to tell them. There were a couple of hours until she was expected, he might as well buy the Chief a pint.

'Did you expect me to refuse?' Ian raised his eyebrows before glancing outside to see if he needed his jacket. A woman was pushing a pram and Ian could see her hair and the hem of her skirt were blowing. He decided he did. 'It's frustrating, this waiting. I hope they don't get held up in traffic.'

There was the usual lunchtime surge of pedestrians as they left their offices and places of work to shop or purchase sandwiches. Clouds raced across the sky leaving patches of blue and revealing the sun at intermittent intervals. 'It's got to be sex.'

'Trust you to think that, but I have to agree with you.' Ian frowned as he waited for a break in the traffic so they could cross the road. 'They're all so damn attractive, but perhaps that's coincidence. Whatever it was I'm pretty certain it started before Kelly Mercer disappeared, when they were all under sixteen.'

'But isn't it odd? *They* were in a position to blackmail whoever it is far more than the other way around.'

114

'If what we suspect is true. We could be way off the mark. Come on, quick.'

Barry took three long strides to catch up with Ian who had darted out between a lorry and a motor bike, an unnecessary risk as there was a crossing twenty yards away.

'Girls these days are mature beyond their years,' Barry continued when they'd got their breath back. 'They'd have known the legal position and a lot of them wouldn't hesitate to use it. If it backfired they could come the innocent bit. Where're we going, by the way?'

'I thought we'd try the Pink Elephant. They're still doing a great lunch trade, apparently.'

Barry made no comment as to the Chief's choice of venue and was not in the least perturbed that it was a gay bar. Many workers from the Town Hall used it, as the place had built up a reputation for excellent food.

They had one drink each and a sandwich, not wishing to stay long in case Richie Howlett made good time.

'Very good,' Ian said when they had finished. The beer was in perfect condition and the sandwich had a hefty filling, plenty of garnish and some crisps on the side of the plate.

They returned to the station to wait.

At a few minutes after three thirty Richie Howlett shepherded Ann Proctor through the revolving doors and across the wide expanse of floor to the counter. The desk sergeant rang the Chief, who came downstairs at once. He smiled reassuringly and asked Richie to take a seat. 'We'll be as quick as we can, son. Do you want some tea while you're waiting?'

'No thanks. Can I come in with Ann?'

'I'm afraid that's not possible. If you change your mind about the tea, have a word with Sergeant Whitelaw here.' Before Richie could say anything more Ian was guiding Ann towards the interview rooms.

Initially he had decided to have DC Gibbons in on the interview but had then opted in favour of a WPC's presence, with himself and Barry asking the questions. It was an unfair technique in view of the girl's obvious fear but a uniform was often more intimidating. They were still not sure if Kelly was safe but during his conversation with Maggie Simpson she had intimated that this was the case. He knew Maggie wanted Ann to tell him because she did not want to break a confidence. 'In here.' Ian held open the door of interview room number 5. The recording equipment was already set up and the WPC stood against the wall at right angles to the door.

Ann's pale face whitened further, giving her an almost blue appearance. She blinked rapidly several times and clasped her hands together as if she was expecting to be handcuffed.

'Have a seat, Miss Proctor.'

She did so, sitting nervously on the edge of it. DS Swan timed his entrance to perfection. Just as Ann was composing herself he flung open the door. She blinked twice more as she jumped like a startled deer on seeing that there were to be two detectives present.

Ian switched on the recording machine and dealt with the usual formalities. Ann said that she understood what was happening and what would later happen to the tapes but was asked to speak up as her voice was barely above a whisper. She recited her full name, age and address, and the interview began.

'Why did you run away, Ann?' Ian asked.

'I don't know really. I was scared.'

'Scared of what?' Ian sat back and folded his arms then unfolded them immediately he realised he was displaying bad body language. He needed the girl to open up, not believe that there was a barrier between them.

'I don't know.'

Ian leaned forward, his hands resting on his knees now. 'I think you do, Ann,' he said mildly, 'and it will be better for everyone if you tell us what it is.' Silence followed this remark. 'Ann, just what is it that frightens you so much?'

'It's what Kelly told me.'

Barry kept his face expressionless and forced himself not to look at the Chief although he had sensed him stiffen imperceptibly.

'When did you speak to Kelly?'

116

Ann's head was bent. She mumbled something which they did not hear.

'When, Ann – when did you speak to her?'

She looked up and met his eyes. Her own were filled with tears. 'Recently,' she said.

'How recent?'

'Just after her mother was killed.'

The release of the tension both Ian and Barry had been experiencing was almost tangible; the atmosphere in the room seemed to change and to become warmer somehow. 'So she's safe?' Ian continued.

Ann explained where she was and what she was doing. 'I wasn't supposed to tell. I promised I wouldn't.'

'I can understand how you feel about that but you must realise you had to tell us. Kelly would understand too.'

Ann nodded as Ian made a written note of the name of the hospital, not that he was likely to forget it now. He smiled and thanked her before standing and leaving the room silently and quite light-footedly for a man of his size. Outside he stopped a passing officer and gave him instructions. When he returned to the interview room Ann Proctor was chewing her nails. He inclined his head towards Barry as a sign that he wished him to continue with the questioning.

'Now we know where Kelly is and that she's all right, but it would be of even more help if you can think of any reason why she went in the first place.'

Colour flooded Ann's face. She seemed childlike and vulnerable yet, at the same time, a desirable woman. Ian began to understand the appeal these girls must have had to whoever had used them. If that was what had happened.

Ann had always known that one day she would have to speak up. Her conscience would not have let her live with the situation. Now she was at the police station it seemed pointless to prolong it. Later, when it was over, she would tell Richie. She inhaled deeply and pushed back her hair with a tired hand. 'I think it was because of my father.' She spoke rapidly, as if she could not wait to be rid of the words.

'Your father?' Barry waited. His hands were clasped loosely on the table. He did not alter his grip.

117

'I didn't tell the truth before. I *was* friendly with Kelly. More than friendly. We grew up together.'

As we suspected, Barry thought, but now was not the time for comment.

'I didn't know, I honestly didn't know anything when she left. But I'd sort of guessed, you see. I couldn't say anything at home. Mum would have been devastated and Dad, well . . .' She paused and gave a small shrug. Ian could imagine Sean Proctor's reaction to any sort of confrontation. 'When Kelly rang she told me everything. I couldn't believe it was her at first. I asked what she would have done if one of my parents had answered and she said she'd have hung up and tried another time. She told me she couldn't come home for the funeral because of Dad, because she was terrified of him.'

'What did she mean by that, Ann?'

Ann took another deep breath. Her face was pale now but she was in control. 'She told me that my father had forced her into having sex with him and that she wasn't the only one.'

'I need to ask you this. When she said sex, did she mean full sexual intercourse?'

'Yes.' Ann looked him full in the eye. 'She said the others didn't seem to care that much, they more or less treated it as a joke. My father gave them money.'

'Do you know any of the others?'

'Kelly told me that Lizzie Conrad and Michelle Short were involved.' Now it was out in the open Ann felt better. Although she did not disbelieve Kelly it was still hard to equate it all with her father. He was vicious and nasty at times and she knew how he treated her mother. But all the same, he was still her dad.

'Why do you think Kelly took it all so much harder?'

'She said she was sure he was obsessed with her, that it wasn't the same with the others. He said he would never let her go, and he was blackmailing her.'

'In what way?'

'She didn't tell me.'

'Do you know where these acts took place?'

'At Kelly's grandmother's place.'

118

Barry nodded. It added up. Enid Mercer spent a lot of her life in hospital and her family would have spare keys. 'All right, let's for a minute assume that what Kelly told you is true. Why do you think that after all this time she's still frightened? She's an adult now. If your father was only interested in young girls she's got nothing to fear.'

'I don't know. My father came in and we had to end the conversation. All she said was that if I was in danger or anything happened to me I could go to Maggie Simpson's place. She made me swear I would never tell anyone about it before she gave me the address.'

'Ann, do you think Kelly's mother found out what had been going on?' Ian took up the questioning.

'I don't know. But if she had, surely she'd have come to you?'

From experience he knew that that was not necessarily the case. 'This isn't an easy question to ask you, but do you think Kelly had an idea that your father may have killed Dee?'

Ann's eyes filled with tears as she nodded slowly. 'I thought so too. I thought if Dee had found out she may have threatened to go to the police, or perhaps she threatened to tell my mother.'

It fitted. Except for one thing. The time gap. If Kelly's reason for disappearing was to do with Sean Proctor's attentions why hadn't Dee come forward at the time? She was apparently happy enough for Kelly to leave home and it was to be supposed she knew her reasons for so doing. It didn't fit, Ian decided as he rapidly changed his opinion. 'If Kelly gave you Miss Simpson's address she presumably thought you were in danger. Why?'

'She didn't say that, she didn't really explain but she thought I might need somewhere to go. She was in quite a state herself. She said she knew Owen couldn't have killed her mother.'

'She knew?' Ian held his breath.

'Oh, I don't mean that. Like, she knew he wouldn't have hurt her. She believed you'd sort it all out without her coming forward.'

A thought crossed Ian's mind. Had Kelly's telephone call to Ann been a cry for help? A way of letting people know where

119

she was without actually admitting to it? Was she now ready to talk to them?

'You'll have to speak to my dad now, won't you?'

'Yes, Ann, I'm afraid we will.'

'Does he have to know I've told you?'

'No, that won't be necessary.' But Ian saw her dilemma. Unless Sean Proctor was particularly stupid he was bound to make the connection between his daughter's disappearance and the line of their questioning. 'I'll arrange for someone to take you home.'

'No.' She stood up, her body rigid. 'I'm not going back there. I'll stay with Richie.'

'That might be for the best.' Ian indicated to the WPC that the escort duty was hers. 'Thank you, Ann. I know how difficult this has been for you.'

'So, what did you make of that?' Ian asked when only he and Barry remained in the room.

'Difficult to know.' A knock on the door interrupted further deliberation. Brenda Gibbons had come to inform them that Kelly Mercer was indeed a nurse, now in her third year of training, and lived in hospital accommodation.

'Good. Let's hope everything else she's told us is true. Come and sit down a minute, Brenda.'

She joined them at the table and listened to an outline of what had taken place, whistling through her teeth when she learned that Proctor's own daughter thought him capable of murder. 'It's certainly a possibility and from what I've discovered these girls, who were all such close friends, claim to have lost touch. It's more a case of wishing to forget the past, if you ask me. And who can blame them? But I'm still not sure how any of it coincides with the murder.'

'You're right. Logically, just because Proctor's got a thing about young girls doesn't mean he's into killing people.' Ian rubbed his forehead. All of a sudden he felt unbelievably tired. 'What I can't understand is why Kelly suddenly decides to make contact again. If Ann didn't know what was going on, why tell her now? It's not the act of a friend, not unless she really did fear for her safety. Ah, well, let's see where we go from here.'

120

For several minutes they sat in silence. Barry leaned forward, his elbows folded and on the table. He nodded slowly. 'Mm, and it probably means that the photograph which Derek Cavanagh found and which caused him so much trouble was presumably one of the ones Proctor took – but why should Kelly be in possession of it?'

'Perhaps she got hold of it without his knowledge, maybe he gave it to her, but I think she took it to school to show Maggie Simpson, to prove to her that she wasn't making up some hysterical story.'

'Would a girl do that, embarrass herself in that way?'

Brenda thought about it. 'Yes. I suspect a lot would if it was the only way to get out of a situation. But, remember, Simpson said Kelly refused to say who the man was.'

'Is it true? She's a great one for confidentiality.'

'I'm positive it is. She'd protect the girls or women but I'm damn sure she'd want the man responsible punished.'

'Good point. I wonder how Proctor was blackmailing her?'

'We'll ask him, shall we?' The Chief stood, towering over the table. He smiled. It had been a successful day even if all they had gained was the knowledge that Kelly was alive and well and had not, as Miss Simpson feared, taken to prostitution. It would be interesting to hear what she had to say but first, out of courtesy, he would contact the Met and inform them of his intentions. Tomorrow he would drive down and see her. Three years into her training Kelly would not be running again. He got Brenda to contact the hospital where she spoke to the sister on the ward where Kelly was currently working. The sister confirmed she would be on duty the following day and was requested not to say anything about the call. Proctor, he decided, could wait another day. So far they only had hearsay upon which to act. He wanted it from the horse's mouth.

An hour later, without consciously recognising what they were doing, the trio automatically headed up the High Street in the direction of the Feathers. The sky had cleared and a warm sun shone on their heads, highlighting the thinness of Barry's hair and the gleam of Brenda's. 'Soon be summer,' Ian said cheerfully as a surge of optimism flooded through him.

Brenda grinned back. She, too, was feeling optimistic as she had agreed to meet Andrew again at the weekend. When he did not put in an appearance in the pub she was surprised at the extent of her disappointment.

9

Superintendent Thorne had no option but to agree that Ian's journey to London was necessary. 'You're right, we need her story first. Well done.'

Ian knew the praise was not for him alone and would pass it on when the time came.

'It could be there's no more to it than a few foolish school-girls getting involved in something they were better out of, but if the Mercer girl was so afraid she missed her mother's funeral then there's really cause for concern.' Mike Thorne sighed. 'Let's hope this isn't all a game.'

But neither of them believed it was.

Ian had toyed with the idea of taking the train from Ricken-ham Green but the branch line service was unreliable. Instead, he drove into Ipswich, parked in a long-stay car-park and caught a direct service to Liverpool Street. Once there he merged with the last of the rush-hour stragglers, not in the least envious of their metropolitan lives. A day trip to London was his limit now although when he was younger he had loved the city.

He managed to find a seat on the tube and sat with his long legs tucked out of the way of fellow travellers as the train hurtled through the tunnels. 'Mind the gap. Mind the gap', an automated voice instructed officiously at several of the sta-tions. He managed to hold claustrophobia at bay until the journey finally came to an end.

The ward sister had said it would be in order for him to talk to Kelly whilst she was on duty but Ian had decided to wait until it was time for her lunch break. No matter how private a room was provided, Ian was aware of what busy places hospitals are and that the chances of not being interrupted were slight. Her break lasted for forty-five minutes; if Kelly was as conscientious as the sister had said she was then she would not want to be late back from it and that might be inducement enough to get everything over with quickly. He had no doubts that she would talk: he had enough ammunition to ensure that she did.

Ian stopped at the main reception desk and asked directions to the ward which were given with a reminder that he only had to follow the arrowed signs. He found his destination without difficulty. He knew what Kelly looked like from the pictures of her in the house where she had lived in Culver Road. There was an hour and a quarter to kill before twelve fifteen and he was tempted to get the interview over with. Standing in the corridor trying to make up his mind, he was almost run over by a trolley which was being pushed with what, to him, seemed great speed. The patient was fully conscious and chatting to his porters and Ian wondered how he wasn't too dizzy to speak. He turned around and headed back to the main stairwell where he hoped the cafeteria would be signposted. It was and he headed towards it, wondering if Kelly Mercer had changed during the past three years. He felt sure he would still recognise her, her looks were so striking.

At five past twelve and with two cups of coffee inside him he was seated on the narrow bench in the corridor outside the ward.

When Kelly Mercer pushed open the swing door he knew her immediately. Her long pale hair was pinned up under her cap, emphasising the curves of her face. Her mouth was full and wide and hinted at sensual petulance. She wore no make-up and only tiny gold studs in her ears. 'Miss Mercer?' Ian stood, his identification already on display.

'Oh, God.' Her hand flew to her mouth.

'No.' A slow smile formed. 'Only a chief inspector.'

Kelly relaxed fractionally. 'I thought this would happen one day. I suppose in a way I wanted it to. Do you want to come to my room?'

He inferred nothing more from this than that it was an invitation to talk in private; it was possibly where Kelly spent

123

her lunch break every day, away from the bustle of the hospital. 'If you don't mind. It might make things easier.'

They made their way out of the main building and crossed an almost full car-park. Ahead was one of the nurses' homes. It was square and modern and there were different curtains hanging in every window. Perhaps they had to provide them themselves. Kelly led him up the concrete stairs and along the passageway to her room. It was larger than Ian had anticipated but there were no signs that the occupant was feminine. It seemed that Kelly had no need to impose her personality upon her surroundings. She sat on the bed leaving Ian the wooden chair in the corner.

'I shall regret it to the day I die,' she began without preamble. 'No matter what the circumstances I should have said a proper goodbye to my mum.' The sadness showed and Ian noticed the dark circles beneath her eyes. She had spent many nights crying.

'Kelly, did you know we were looking for you?'

She sat calmly, her hands resting in her lap, every man's dream of a blonde angelic nurse. 'Yes, I did,' she admitted.

'You've caused us an awful lot of work, you know.' He said it without rancour, aware of the depth of her grief and fear, emotions complicated by guilt and regret.

'I'm sorry. Was it Ann who told you where I was?'

'Yes.'

'Ah, I thought so. Maybe that's why I rang her,' she added softly. 'I can't go back there, to Rickenham.'

'If you answer my questions truthfully there may not be any need for you to do so.'

She nodded her acceptance of this statement. 'I'm sorry, aren't I supposed to offer you tea? They do it all the time on television.' She gave a mirthless laugh. 'Just like we do in hospital.'

'If you're having some.'

He recognised the delaying tactic but the girl had a lot to think about. It was also her lunch break, he could not deny her a drink.

She filled the kettle from the small wash-basin and reached for the two mugs which were on the shelf above it. The tea-bags were stored in a patterned tin which had once held chocolate biscuits and had probably been a gift from a grateful patient.

'Milk and sugar?'

'Just milk, please.'

When it was ready Ian took a sip from his mug allowing Kelly time to sit on the edge of her bed. 'Ann told us you were frightened. What is it that scares you so much you didn't come back for the funeral?'

Kelly did not flinch. She had steeled herself for the question. 'Sean Proctor.'

'Why?'

'Because I think he killed my mother and I think he'd kill me too.'

'Then why didn't you contact us?'

She shook her head. 'I thought you'd find out. I was so bloody sure you'd see it couldn't possibly have been Owen. He loved her, you've no idea how much he loved her.'

'Just one simple telephone call would've done.'

'I know that. Don't speak to me as if I'm a child. I'm sorry.' Her anger evaporated as quickly as it had arisen. 'You're right, of course, I should have contacted someone. He'd never have found out. I was just waiting to hear you'd made a mistake. Nothing happened. I knew then that I needed to do something. I spoke to Ann. I've known her all my life. I knew she'd come to you or at least do something to draw your attention to him. She's as honest as they come, she wouldn't have protected that bastard.'

Ian was pleased she was angry; it was better than being afraid and if she was angry enough she might be prepared to stand up in court. 'Look, we know about the other girls and we know . . .' He stopped, aware of the way the conversation was heading. 'Kelly, would you do me a great favour? Would you come back with me? I'll guarantee protection the whole time. The thing is, I can't ask you the things I need to know. Not here, not just you and me in your room. No one need know you're in Rickenham. Would you do that? When your shift's finished, of course.'

For a second or two her eyes were clouded then she came to a decision. 'This can't go on. I want to get it over with. If you'll speak to Sister I'd prefer it if we went now.'

'That's fine by me.' Ian could pull rank if necessary. This

125

was, after all, a serious investigation but he hoped it would not be necessary. 'I'll go over to the ward now and sort it out.'

He turned his back as he saw the first tears glisten in Kelly's eyes. 'I'm doing this for Owen, you understand.'

'I know. You get changed while I nip across to the hospital.' He hoped it would not cause too much of a problem on the ward.

The sister said she supposed she had no choice in the matter but to agree. She was professional enough to remain reticent and, in return, Ian reassured her that Kelly had done nothing wrong; he left it at that because he was unsure how much, or little, the hospital staff knew of the girl's background. 'We'll have her back in time for work tomorrow.'

'Tomorrow's no problem, Chief Inspector, it's the start of Student Nurse Mercer's off duty.' The sister's sigh expressed regret that he couldn't have waited a day before turning up.

Ian left the ward and retraced his steps. He had been idiotic to imagine he could get all the details from Kelly in forty-five minutes but things had turned out better than he had expected. At least she had supplied enough information to warrant him taking her back.

Kelly was in the middle of the room when he returned. Her uniform was on a hanger hooked over the handle of the sliding door of the minute wardrobe. She had changed into jeans and a long, loose jumper which concealed her figure. Her hair was unpinned and flowing around her shoulders. There was a slight kink in it where it had been twisted into a knot. 'Do I need to take anything with me?'

Ian calculated it would probably be too late for her to travel back that night. They would have to find her a hostel or somewhere safe because there was no question of her returning to Culver Road. Failing that, there was always Judy Robbins to fall back on. She had a spare bedroom and Kelly would feel extra safe under the roof of a policewoman. 'Yes. I think you'd better pack an overnight bag.'

'What did Sister say?'

'Oh, she was fine. Said it was okay.'

Kelly looked doubtful but pulled out a small hold-all from under the bed into which she put the nightdress which had been under her pillow and some washing things which were beside the basin. No make-up, Ian noticed, and no perfume. 'Do you think you'll need a jacket or something?'

She shook her head and inserted her key in the lock, pulling the door closed behind her.

They left the hospital grounds, Ian carrying the hold-all and wondering how many passers-by would assume he had come to collect his daughter to take her home for her days off. He thought about hailing a taxi then decided it was best to give Kelly time to adjust to the idea that she was going home.

On the train to Ipswich they made small talk for the first part of the journey, carefully avoiding any reference to the reason for their being together, then they lapsed into silence as they neared their destination. Kelly stared out of the window but Ian doubted if she saw anything other than what was going on in her mind.

'My car's at Ipswich station,' he told her, letting her know that she would not have the ordeal of walking through the streets of Rickenham. 'I'll drive us straight to headquarters.'

He was rewarded with a half-smile and tried to gauge the effect the full works would have on a man. In the car he asked if she wanted to listen to some music but she said she preferred the quiet. Taking the hint he made no attempt to talk to her.

During their progression from the foyer to the interview room heads turned. Within minutes everyone knew that Kelly Mercer had been found.

'Are you ready to tell me about it?' Richie Howlett crouched in front of Ann who was seated in his shabby armchair. His light brown hair, cut short, accentuated his slightly protruding ears and his brow was creased with worry.

'I can't. Not just yet. I will, though, I promise, after they've spoken to Kelly.'

'Don't you trust me?'

'It's not that, Richie, honestly it isn't.' She looked away, not wishing to witness the pain in his eyes. They had had no secrets; it was the first thing she had ever kept from him.

'I was frantic, you know. You're not being fair to me, Ann, I thought it was because you didn't want to see me any more but you were too afraid to tell me.'

'How can you say that? You know it was you I wanted to come and get me.'

Richie nodded. 'In that case it has to be to do with your parents. That's why you didn't want to go home, isn't it?' He didn't mean to pressurise her, she looked tired and drawn, but he did feel he deserved an answer. Ann felt so too.

'All right, I'll tell you although I'm not sure how much of it is true.'

He listened without comment until she had finished speaking. There were no recriminations, no shocked outrage. He put his arms around her and said, 'Oh, Ann, you poor little thing. They'll know where you are though – what if they come here?'

'Just say I'm not in. I can stay, can't I?'

'I've already said so.'

'I know, but now . . .'

'It makes no difference, you haven't done anything. I'll make us a drink then I think you ought to get some sleep. Will you be going back to work?'

Ann had not given the matter any thought. It might be that there was no job waiting for her as she had not informed her employers of her plans. Her mother had also taken time off, but they would understand the reason for that. If she did go back she could not avoid seeing her mother as they shared four of the same days each week.

Ann drank her tea then gratefully rolled beneath the duvet on Richie's single bed. To her surprise she felt her eyelids drooping and drifted into sleep almost at once.

'I want to know why she won't come home.'

'I don't know why, Sean, I'm as much in the dark as you are. I expect it's probably because she's had enough. You know how sensitive she can be, the police have probably scared her.'

'I'll bloody well complain if that's the case. It's harassment,

128

that's what it is. Why can't they leave the girl alone? She's told them everything she knows. Why should they think she knows where Kelly is when no one else around here does?'

'Come here, love.' Eileen reached out and put her arms around him, pressing up close against his body. If only she didn't love him, if only she could look at him objectively, without desire, then life would be so different. She had envied Dee her strength, her ability to live her life by the standards she had set for herself. If she was as strong she would have left Sean years ago. Ann had always been her excuse; she had convinced herself that a child needed the stability of two parents and, despite his other faults, Sean had always been a good father. I know why he hits me, she thought, I didn't need to be a genius to work that out. But knowing did not help, there was nothing she could do about it, no way in which she could turn back the clock. She could live with it; the one thing she could not live with was with other people knowing.

Sean moved against her and her legs trembled. She kissed him on the mouth as she braced herself for the first slap.

'Will you be all right here for a few minutes?'

Kelly glanced around the bleak interview room and nodded. Her hold-all was beneath the table. Ian pulled out a chair for her and she sat down. 'I'll get something sent up from the canteen. Is there anything you don't like?' He had offered her food on the train but she had only accepted a cup of coffee.

'I'm not hungry.'

'We'll see.' He would get her something light, a sandwich and some tea. The sight of food might make her change her mind. He did not want her to pass out with hunger. She had already been on her feet for four and a quarter hours when he first encountered her and she had had nothing but a couple of drinks since. 'And something to read? There's usually some magazines lying around.' He left the room but did not close the door. He did not want her to feel she was a prisoner. A WPC was sent to keep her company for the ten or fifteen minutes it would take Ian to get organised.

Brenda Gibbons was in the general office. Seated at a desk she had a bemused smile on her face as she listened to whatever someone on the other end of the telephone was saying. 'I'll have to go now,' she said when she saw the Chief. 'See you later. Sir?' She swiftly replaced the receiver.

'I want you to go along and put the squeeze on Lizzie Conrad. I've just checked, she's on duty at the Duke of Clarence this evening until ten. Tell her we've got Kelly here and then put it to her that we know what went on between her and Sean Proctor.'

'But – '

Ian held up a hand to prevent any argument. 'I know, we don't know that yet, but I want this tied up in one go. I want to be able to make an arrest where there's no hint of doubt. And, if the little Kelly's told me is true, then these girls might be in danger if Proctor gets wind of what we're on to. Where's Sergeant Swan?'

'He's got the afternoon off to take Lucy to the clinic.'

'Oh no!'

'It's all right, there's nothing wrong as far as I know, it's just the usual routine check-up.'

'Thank goodness for that.' Ian did not think either of them would get over a second miscarriage so quickly after the first. 'All right, in that case will you do me a favour? Get on to Tyneside and ask if they'd mind doing the honours with Michelle Short. You'd better give them the whole story. Let me know as soon as they come back to us. All we need is a corroborative statement. Oh, and Judy Robbins, is she about today?'

'I haven't seen her but I think she's on patrol duty with Constable Geer.'

'Thanks.' Ian used the phone on Brenda's desk to contact the duty officer only to learn that Judy had finished her shift and had gone. He had to look up her home number which was one, for some reason, he could never remember, unlike when she had lived in the flat. It was almost two years since she had moved into the bungalow which was her father's legacy but he rarely needed to speak to her off duty now. Once she used to come around and look after Mark. Strange, he thought, as he listened to the ringing tone, Judy would have made a wonderful mother but she was leaving it a bit late. There wasn't even a regular man in her life. But Ian was unaware that although Judy loved other people's children she had no desire to produce any of her own.

Brenda Gibbons, long hair swinging to the rhythm of her hips, threaded her way between the desks as she heard the Chief ask Judy if she was doing anything that evening. She grinned. Poor Judy's babysitting days weren't over, she was going to be landed with Kelly Mercer.

'Long day?'

'Too damn long.' Ian sank into his armchair and kicked off his shoes. He had not stopped for a drink on the way home, a fact upon which Moira commented when he had kissed her and she couldn't taste beer. She offered to pour him one now. 'Is there any left?'

'Yes, I got some more at lunchtime.'

Ian preferred his Adnam's bitter in the pub but occasionally he'd sip a glassful at home. Moira bought it in two-litre plastic bottles from the off-licence or the supermarket.

'Have you eaten?'

Ian frowned. Had he? No, not since breakfast, no wonder his stomach was rumbling. Because Kelly had declined the offer of food on the train he had not bothered to get anything for himself. After that there had been no time to think about eating.

'Obviously not. There's some cold meat, I can do you some chips to go with it.'

The fan of lines around his eyes deepened as he laughed. 'Do I look that much in need of sustenance?' Moira tried to give him plenty of healthy food, the benefits of which were proved by her own figure. Unfortunately Ian favoured anything which had a high cholesterol content and for Moira to offer chips suggested he needed a bit of comfort. 'Go on, then,' he said, 'spoil me.'

Whilst she prepared the makeshift meal he read the paper then, when she called out that it was ready, he went to the kitchen to eat. It was already after ten. 'That's better,' he said as he placed his knife and fork together on the plate. 'I'll give that half an hour to go down, then I'm for bed.'

Moira added his plate to other crockery which was in the dishwasher. This piece of equipment was a recent addition to the Roper household, one purchased out of Moira's salary; she wondered how she had coped without it in the days when Mark was little and she had spent hours baking. Because their meals were irregular and Ian sometimes ate at work it was simplest to stack it and switch it on only when it was full. She did so now and listened to the hiss of water as it filled before beginning its cycle.

Ian poured a second drink and a glass of dry white wine for his wife. It was warm and peaceful in the kitchen with only the gentle background noises of the dishwasher. Outside, through the windows over which the curtains were never drawn, was the blackness of the night. At the back of the house the traffic sounds were muted. Somewhere, quite near-by, they heard the bark of a fox. They both smiled.

Moira joined him at the table where most of their serious conversations took place. 'How did it go?' She studied Ian over the rim of her glass. As always, he had rung her to warn her he would be late, that the Mercer girl was at the station and he had no idea what time she could expect him. Now he was home and she knew he would need to talk about the events of the day.

'It's quite unbelievable. Once we'd spoken to Kelly we followed up the other girls, Michelle Short and Lizzie Conrad, and they confirmed that they had had under-age sex with Proctor. Their only concern was how it might affect their futures if it came out. Anyway, that's not important for the minute. Kelly said that it all began when she was about eleven. She was always round at the Proctors' place. If she was alone with him he'd pick her up and cuddle her et cetera but she was too young to see anything wrong with it. Then on one of the occasions her grandmother was in hospital Dee had called in at the bungalow for something and discovered a small leak. She rang Kelly, who was at home, and asked her to go around to the Proctors' to see if Sean would fix it. She didn't want the place flooded. He agreed and Kelly went with him because she had the other spare key. This was a Saturday evening, Dee had been on her way to work.'

'Leaving Kelly alone?'

'She was fourteen by then and the Proctors were just down the road. Kelly admitted that she found him attractive, but, more than that, she'd been brought up to do as she was told. When Proctor demanded a drink she produced her grand-mother's brandy, knowing she wouldn't mind because the man was doing her a favour. Proctor was making Kelly laugh, she was enjoying herself, and this was probably why she allowed him to persude her to have some of the brandy her-self. She wasn't used to it. She had no idea what half a tumbler would do. When he made his move it was too late. She tried to resist but she didn't have the strength. Afterwards he told her that what she'd done was against the law and that if she told anyone they'd both go to prison. Later, of course, she realised it wasn't true but at the time there was no one she could ask. He was doubly blackmailing her because he also said that if she didn't comply with his wishes he'd tell her mother.'

'Why didn't she let him tell her? Why did she allow it to continue?'

'Because she was young and foolish and couldn't have borne her mother's disapproval. She and Dee were unusually close. Besides, Proctor also threatened her physically. You have to remember that Kelly wasn't like other girls, most of them would have laughed at him or told an adult. In fact, they probably wouldn't have got into the situation to begin with.'

'The poor kid. She couldn't even confide in her mother.'

'Precisely. And for the same reasons she couldn't or wouldn't let anyone else know. He'd got a hold over her she had no idea how to break.'

'And the others?'

'He started asking her if she had any friends who were inter-ested in earning a little extra money. Kelly saw this as a way out. If she provided enough distractions he might leave her alone. She doesn't remember how she talked them round but some kids that age are avaricious enough to do almost any-thing.'

133

'So far, so good. But why wait until she was sixteen to take it into her head to leave home?'

'That's the crunch. Kelly was illegitimate. Well, most people either knew or guessed that, but Dee thought it was time to tell her daughter who her father was. Sixteen always seems to be the age for such revelations. Don't ask me why.' Ian paused. He could feel Moira's eyes on him.

'Oh, don't tell me Proctor was her father?'

Ian nodded. 'Unbelievable, isn't it? Mind you, he didn't know. As soon as Dee told Kelly she became hysterical. She knew then that she would have to let her mother know what had been going on. I can't imagine what it must have been like in that household that day, but it can't have been easy for either of them.'

'But she didn't go to the police.'

'No. Kelly had been through two bad experiences, Dee wanted to protect her from any more. Just think what a court appearance would have done to a girl like that. And even though she would have remained unnamed, it would have been in the press. It doesn't take much to put two and two together. Anyway, between them they arranged for her to go away. A pre-training place came up at the hospital where she still works and Kelly took it.'

'I might be being thick, but how could Dee have befriended Eileen knowing that Sean was the father of her own child?'

'Ah, well, that was the usual story. Dee wasn't living in Culver Road when they met. Proctor led her to believe he was single, and he did a disappearing trick before she'd even found out she was pregnant. Dee saw there was no future in making a fuss, tracking him down, and guessed she'd be better off living off the state until she could find work. Once Kelly was born she was rehoused and that's when she found out who her neighbours were to be. There was no taking up of things where they'd been left off and, strangely, Dee found she got on well with Eileen.'

'But afterwards? When she knew what the man had been doing to Kelly? How could she stay there?'

'As soon as Kelly was safely out of the way she confronted him. He was completely shattered when he learned the truth.

134

Dee told Kelly he had broken down completely when she also told him she knew what had been going on. He wanted to find the girl, to somehow try to put things right, but Dee knew that was an impossibility, nothing could repair the damage he'd already done.'

'Yes, but I don't think I could have remained in the same street.' Moira was indignant.

'You have to remember by that time she'd met Owen, she was happy and Kelly was safe. It makes a lot of difference to your perspective, things like that. She'd coped all those years alone and she was rewarded with a man she loved and who loved her in return. His being there made everything easier to cope with. And Proctor was contrite. He made endless attempts to trace Kelly, to make it up to her, though God knows how he intended doing that.'

'Even accepting that, why didn't Kelly come home for the funeral?'

'She still didn't feel safe from him. Why should she now there was no one to take her side? She knew he'd been trying to find her, Dee had said so, but she didn't trust his motives for wanting to. She believed that we'd discover the truth, that Kerslake would go free without her interference. And, of course, she thought Proctor had killed her mother because she was about to tell Eileen.' Ian held up a hand. 'I know, after all that time it was illogical, but I can see how the girl's mind was working.'

'I thought you said mother and daughter didn't keep in touch?'

'I said we didn't find anything in the house to suggest it. They did though, there were regular telephone conversations and letters. Kelly's were addressed to her grandmother's house.'

'What for?'

'Because the postman who does Culver Road plays cards with Proctor and the Mercers were terrified that he might ask him where her letters were postmarked.'

Moira snorted. 'That's a bit far-fetched. London's not exactly a hamlet.'

'No, but think about it. Proctor knew, as everyone did, how fond of children Kelly was. It wouldn't take much effort to work out that the children's hospital was in that district.'

135

'Ian, has it occurred to you that it still might be Kerslake, that he killed Dee because he learned who Kelly's father was and thought she was seeing him behind his back, or he'd found out what he was doing to Kelly and was disgusted with her for not reporting it?'

'We've spoken to him again. He now admits he knew where Kelly was but he had sworn to Dee he would never tell anyone.'

'Not even after he'd been arrested?'

'No. There was a hell of a lot of loyalty in that family. Even the grandmother denied she knew of Kelly's whereabouts. Anyway, I don't think Kerslake knew of the real reason for Kelly leaving but he was happy enough to go along with whatever Dee said. To be honest, I think he'd have accepted anything from her as long as he didn't lose her.'

'He did this at the risk of his own future.' Moira was watching the wine in her glass as she swirled it.

'Owen Kerslake no longer considers himself to have a future, not without Dee.'

'Neither would I if anything happened to you.'

Ian reached across the table and took her hand. There were no words to explain how he felt about Moira. 'Come on, let's go to bed.'

'What'll happen to Owen?' she asked as she checked the back door.

'I don't know. We're still not convinced that Proctor's the murderer. Everything points to him, but then, everything seemed to point to Kerslake.'

Upstairs they took it in turns to use the bathroom then started to undress. 'Just because both Kelly and her grandmother believe he's innocent doesn't make it a fact.' Ian sighed and shook his head. His mind was no longer functioning. He pulled off his tie and threw it over the back of the padded chair in front of the dressing-table. His jacket followed. Moira had never managed to get him to hang it up. 'Enough shop talk. Get into bed and give your old man a cuddle.'

Moira did so. Three minutes later she extricated her arm from beneath the dead weight of his sleeping body.

'We've got their written statements,' Brenda Gibbons announced next morning. 'Tyneside faxed us through a copy of Michelle Short's.'

DS Barry Swan was amazed at the progress that had been made during his brief absence and wondered if he ought to take a few more afternoons off. Not that any of it led any closer to proving Kerslake's innocence. It was not the way they should be looking at things. Having arrested and charged the man they had completed their duties, yet here they were trying to reverse the situation. They were to interview Proctor, who would have to take his chance as far as his family were concerned. Ann did not wish to return home but it would not surprise him if his wife stuck by him. 'Where's the girl?'

'Kelly? She spent the night with Judy Robbins. She's travelling back to London today and Judy's going to see her to the train. She took her up to her mother's grave first thing, apparently.'

Barry nodded. Judy's abrasiveness had always irritated him, that and her lack of respect for his being male, but he had to accept she was marvellous in such situations. 'We'd better put in an appearance at the briefing.'

Markham was on his feet. 'This is the address of the insurance company he works for,' he said, referring to Sean Proctor. 'He'd already left for work by the time we got to the house. He likes to get in before the others, apparently. Mrs Proctor was also out. She starts at eight. I've checked and they're both in their respective places of employment which means they don't suspect that we suspect.'

'Okay, send someone over to pick him up.' The Chief ended the briefing and the party disbanded in various directions with the exception of one or two detectives who remained at their desks and began to make telephone calls or call up information on their computer screens. Ian could not imagine what must be going through Kerslake's mind. After their last visit he must realise that the police were not entirely happy about his arrest. For the time being there were more pressing matters to consider.

Barry joined Ian in his office whilst they waited for the arrival of Sean Proctor. They sat quietly smoking, saying little, as they contemplated why a man needed to choose very young girls to fulfil his sexual needs. When he did arrive they did not rush themselves to interview him. The officer who had brought him in said he was full of bluster and indignation at having been dragged from his place of work and had protested strongly at his treatment, threatening them with a complaint.

'Let him cool his heels,' Ian instructed PC Fellows. 'Make sure someone's with him, but no conversation is to take place. We'll give him fifteen minutes.' Ian knew how unnerving it was to be seated under guard in an impersonal room, especially when the person guarding you refused to acknowledge anything you said.

When the apportioned time was up they made their way grimly down to the interview room corridor.

'What's the meaning of this?' Proctor demanded to know, standing immediately upon their entry. 'You can't leave us alone at home and now you've got the nerve to pester me at my office.'

'Sit down, please, Mr Proctor. We won't detain you longer than is necessary but there are a couple of matters we'd like to clear up.' Ian's manner was urbane and guaranteed to defuse Proctor's hectoring.

'I want a solicitor,' he said, but more quietly as he resumed his seat. There was a sheen of sweat on his forehead and he ran a finger around the neck of his collar as if the room was overheated. Ian could smell his expensive aftershave.

'Do you think you need one?' The question was put with feigned surprise. 'We only want to ask you some questions. You haven't been arrested.'

The words must have reassured him because Proctor sat back in his chair, his breathing steadier. He was well built but other than that neither Ian nor Barry saw what it was about him that made young girls willing to go along with him. His lips were on the full side and his smoothly shaved jowls were fleshy. There was, however, something compelling about his eyes, something that was almost magnetic.

Noticing his relaxed posture Ian decided to plunge straight in. 'Before we start I'd like to inform you that we have taken statements from three girls: Lizzie Conrad, Michelle Short and . . .' He left a minute pause before adding, 'Kelly Mercer.'

'Kelly?' The redness left Proctor's face. Shock had turned it white and made his hands shake. He clasped them in his lap as he tried to gain control of himself. Ian knew then that he had him. 'Oh, God. Where is she? Please tell me where she is.'

Ian ignored the question. 'These three girls have all told us the same thing, that you encouraged, then bribed them to have sexual intercourse with you at a time when they were all under the age of consent.'

Proctor laughed. 'Girls will say anything to get attention. I'm a happily married man, Chief Inspector, why should I want to risk my marriage and a possible jail sentence?'

'You tell me.'

'My God, there's no limit to it, is there? Ask my wife and daughter, they'll tell you what a happy family we are.'

'But your daughter is no longer living at home, Mr Proctor, is she?'

'How the hell did you know that? If you've been pestering her again as well I'll – '

'Why did she leave?' Ian interrupted as if there had been no outburst.

Proctor pulled a white cotton handkerchief from his jacket pocket and wiped his brow. 'Boyfriend trouble. She and Richie Howlett had some kind of row. It happens. They're all right again now.'

Ian had advised Ann that if her parents questioned her this might be the best line to take but he did not know if she had contacted her parents or if this was Proctor's way of covering up. He let it go and returned to the subject he was interested in. 'Are you saying that three girls, all in different parts of the country, are lying?'

The man seemed to shrink inside his grey striped suit. He sighed then stared at the wall ahead of him. 'All right. But they were willing enough. So help me, I didn't force them, I never needed to. And it was only once.'

'With Lizzie and Michelle. What about Kelly?'

'More than once.'

'How many times?'

'I didn't keep a count,' he replied sarcastically.

'No need, was there? You were safe enough because you were blackmailing her.'

'No, I wasn't.' Proctor moved to the edge of his seat and rested his elbows on the table. Over the aftershave Ian could smell his fear. 'I simply said she must not tell anyone.'

'Because you were her father.'

'Oh shit!' He sat perfectly still, knowing he was going to be charged. 'I didn't know and that's the truth. Neither did Kelly. Do you think I'd have . . .' He stopped. No doubt they would think he'd have done it anyway.

'Were there other girls?'

'Only two.'

'We need their names. They might need counselling.'

'My God,' Proctor spluttered, looking for an opportunity to defend himself. 'If you'd met them you'd know how ridiculous it sounds. They could have passed for eighteen any day of the week. And I wasn't the first.'

'We shall meet them. Their names, please.'

'Will my family need to know?' he asked when he had supplied the names.

'I can't see any way of avoiding it. Sergeant Swan will read you your rights.'

Having done so he and Ian left Proctor under the auspices of the PC, who had remained standing silently behind them throughout the exchange.

'Now what?' Barry asked as they stood at the end of the long corridor in a position which made passing difficult. They were oblivious to the nuisance they were creating.

'When he's had a break and drunk his tea we'll start again.

140

He's scared. He coughed too easily for my liking. I get the feeling he's prepared to hold his hand up to this to distract us from more serious matters.'

'I don't. But I think you think that's how you'd like it to be.'

'Damn you, Barry. You're right. Who am I trying to convince?' Ian shook his head. 'C'mon, let's get some coffee.' He strode off leaving Barry, with his shorter legs, to catch him up.

Eileen Proctor knew that her daughter was staying with Richie. Ann had telephoned to say where she was and that she'd be in touch. It had seemed better to do that than have her parents coming round every five minutes. When Sean did not arrive home after work at his usual time she gave him another hour in case he had been in a meeting or got held up in traffic before dialling Richie's number. She was worried, but not unduly so. Sean normally rang if he was going to be delayed but there was the chance he'd had an accident. 'Have you seen your father?' she asked when Richie put Ann on the line.

'No. Should I have?'

'He's not here. I thought he might have called in to try to talk you into coming home.'

'No, I haven't seen him.'

Ten minutes later, as Eileen was pacing between the front room and the kitchen wondering what steps she ought to take, the telephone rang. 'I was so worried. Where are you, love?' Her relief at hearing Sean's voice was immense.

'I'm at the police station. I can't talk now. I've been arrested. They said I could let you know. Don't worry. Everything'll be all right.'

Eileen replaced the receiver slowly and took several deep breaths. Those girls, she thought, they've caught up with him at last. Tears filled her eyes as she saw it might all stop now, because the police would always be watching him. They might make a real go of things at last. Hope was mixed with the dread of people knowing. The one thing she had been able to prevent might now be taken out of her hands. The press would make much of it, she was sure of that. Suddenly her legs felt weak. She sat on the plastic-covered settee and began to shake. They might not make a go of it, it might be worse if Sean was thwarted. She knew that he hit her because she was no longer young, that she could not provide him with whatever the girls did and that he could only make love to her when he felt he was dominant. Would the slaps turn to punches? He had never marked her and she did not mind his roughness, but she could not bear the way he looked at her body when she was naked. It was so unfair. She was neither fat nor thin and had worn better than many women her age.

'How did they know?' she whispered just as the answer came into her head. Ann. Had Ann found out, maybe through one of her friends, and was that why she had refused to come home? 'I love him,' she said as if she was excusing his, and her own, behaviour to the protected furniture. 'I can't help it.'

Her self-pity gave way to thoughts of her daughter. How would Sean react if he found out it was she who had given him away? One thing was certain, he would never get away with hurting Ann. With an effort Eileen composed herself. She must prepare Ann for what lay ahead. Together they would get through it. Several times her hand hovered over the telephone receiver before she finally picked it up and dialled the number. 'Do you think you could come over for an hour?' she asked. 'Something's happened, something I can't discuss over the phone.'

'I don't want to. Richie and I are going out.'

'Please, love, it's very important. It concerns your father.' Eileen heard Ann's indrawn breath and knew that her guess had been right. 'He's not in,' she added persuasively.

'All right. I'll ask Richie to drive me over. He can wait in the car.' She knew her mother would not discuss family problems in front of anyone else, not even Richie.

Richie agreed to run her to her parents' house. 'I'll have a stroll around the park,' he told her as he kissed her on the cheek. She was still pale and he knew she would not be back to her old self until the matter had been resolved. He smiled his encouragement before heading in the direction of the small playing field which abutted the houses on the opposite side of the road. The evening was mild and he could do with the fresh air.

'Mum? Are you all right?' Ann was shocked at Eileen's appearance. Her face was blotchy and her eyes were swollen with crying.

'Yes, I'm okay. I've poured us a drink.'

Ann followed her to the kitchen. Already, even after so short an absence, she felt like a guest in her own home and nothing seemed as familiar as it ought to have done. Eileen rarely touched alcohol and Ann's stomach muscles tightened when she saw the half-bottle of gin. She picked up her glass and ice tinkled against the side as she took the first fortifying sip.

Eileen watched her. How young and innocent she was, and so beautiful that she could have been a model had she so chosen. And now that innocence had been defiled. She pulled out a chair. 'Sit down, love. Oh, listen to me, inviting you to sit down in your own home.'

Ann tried to smile but failed. In retrospect she realised her mother had not looked well for some time. She wondered how much strain she had been living under.

'I may as well come straight to the point. Your father's been arrested.'

'Oh God.' Ann's hand flew to her mouth. She felt she might faint. Kelly was right, her father was a murderer.

'I have to talk to you, Ann, I need you to know that I've known about it for some years. It's bothered me, it really has, but not as much as it should have done. I'd do anything for that man and to keep us together. No one was getting hurt and he was always a wonderful father to – '

'For years? You've known about it for years?' Ann realised she had been wrong, it was not Dee Mercer's murder they were discussing here.

'He's not an evil man, love, he just can't help it. Perhaps he needs someone to talk to.'

'You're saying that you knew all along he was sleeping with young girls, girls like Kelly, friends I went to school with, and you've never done anything about it?'

'Don't be angry with me, darling. I love you both so much.'

Ann slammed her glass on to the formica-topped table and stood up. 'Angry? I'm furious. How did you expect me to feel? Did you think I'd say, Oh, that's all right, as long as we

143

three can pretend we're the perfect nuclear family? They were my *friends*. Didn't it occur to you they might have been miserable or frightened? For all you know he could have ruined their lives. Was it that you really loved him so much or was it because you couldn't bear the thought of everyone knowing you were married to a child molester?' She spat out the final two words.

'Ann, he's not that. That's different. Please. Please don't go. I want you to understand.'

'I do understand, that's why I'm leaving. At least I suppose I can be thankful he never tried to touch me. What would you have done then? Turned a blind eye to protect him?'

'No. I wouldn't, I . . . ' But Eileen could not continue. It was a question she had often asked herself but was unable to answer. She had read of women who did just that but was afraid to admit she might be one of them.

'One more thing,' Ann shouted from the front door. 'Has it ever crossed your mind that pervert might have killed Dee?' The door slammed behind her before Eileen could answer.

'No' she muttered. 'No. Not that. He didn't do that.'

Ann was trembling so much she found it difficult to put one foot in front of the other. Richie was not in his car so she made her way to the park but he was nowhere in sight. She continued to walk, aimlessly, for almost an hour. She was not ready to face anyone. Richie would understand. When he got fed up with waiting he'd knock on her parents' door and realise she wanted to be alone.

She found herself in the town centre without being aware of how she got there and suddenly knew she needed to sit down. The adrenalin had stopped surging round her body and she felt exhausted. It was not her usual practice to go into pubs on her own but there was nowhere nearby but the Feathers. Inside she tried to ignore the other twenty or so customers and made her way to the bar where she purchased a half of cider. Only when she turned to find a table to herself did she notice the pretty detective and the tall, pock-faced man with her.

Brenda Gibbons laid a hand on Andrew's wrist and excused herself before making her way across the room to the table half hidden behind a pillar which Ann had chosen deliberately. She had seen by the girl's expression that she was *au fait* with the news and although Brenda was off duty she felt she could not cold-shoulder her. 'You've heard?' she inquired gently as she stood beside the table. Ann nodded but did not look up. 'I'm sorry.' Brenda's words of sympathy released a valve and Ann began to cry. Her sobs were silent but filled her body; her shoulders heaved as the tears ran down her face. Brenda dug into her shoulder bag and found a clean tissue. 'Here. Use this. Can I get you another drink? Something stronger maybe?'

'No. No, it's all right. I'll be fine. Really.' The sobs were no more than hiccups. She had not touched the drink she already had and recognised that the policewoman was trying to be kind. 'It was just knowing that it was certain, you see. I kept trying to kid myself that Kelly was mistaken.'

'Look, if you need to talk there are people I can put you in touch with.'

'Thank you. But I've got Richie. He's all I need.' And with that she picked up her own handbag and managed a watery smile. 'I think I'll go and find him now. You can have my drink if you want. I haven't touched it.'

Brenda watched her leave then went back to join Andrew. Ann Proctor was young and the resilience of youth would see her through this. Brenda had her own problems with which to contend. She suspected that Andrew Osborne was becoming more than a friend and she was not sure if she was ready for that yet.

'How are we going to approach this?'

'Subtly, to begin with, I think,' Ian replied. 'We'll build up to it slowly, let him think we're only interested in what he's admitted to. You can kick off, Barry.'

Sean Proctor had been given a meal and a drink and the opportunity to telephone his wife. He had also been offered the services of a solicitor which now he had decided to accept. Barry had rung the duty solicitor who had promised to be there within the hour and who had kept to his word. Solicitors, whose aim it is to get their clients off or to mitigate their case, and the police, whose aim is to get a conviction, do not always see eye to eye. To Ian's mind barristers were another matter. They were trained to use the law to their own ends, to turn words around and save their clients on legal technicalities. There were few lawyers of either persuasion Ian begrudgingly admitted to liking although he respected quite a few. Peter Robson was not such a man, but here Ian was not alone in his opinion. Robson was generally disliked, even by his clients, although he got results. He was short and overweight to such an extent that his loud suits bulged threateningly around his sausage-like limbs. His sandy hair was thin and greasy and he had an irritating habit of sucking at the ends of his overlong ginger moustache. There was little pigmentation in his blue eyes and he exuded aggression. Robson was one of the few men whom no one could accredit with a redeeming feature. There was nothing Ian could do about it, it was Robson's turn on the rota.

'Ah, Chief Inspector, we meet again.' Robson, several inches shorter than Ian, managed to convey the impression that he was looking him up and down from an equal height. 'What have you got for me this time?'

'Sean Proctor. White male. Age forty-three. Married, one grown-up daughter.' Ian went through the charge blandly, refusing to rise to the bait. 'We now need to question him further, on another matter. He has requested the presence of a solicitor but does not have one of his own, nor was he able to name anyone he would like to represent him.'

Robson smiled, showing two pointed teeth. He was not in the least offended by the obvious way Ian had implied that that was the only reason Robson was anywhere on the premises. 'Then let's go and see Mr Proctor, shall we?'

DCI Roper, DS Swan and Peter Robson LlB walked briskly to where Proctor was still sitting with an empty tray on the table in front of him. Ian nodded to the PC who came forward and removed it, placing it on the floor outside the door of the interview room.

Proctor had relaxed a little, maybe because it was a relief to have things out in the open or maybe because he had a full stomach. He had cleared the plate, which had contained cottage pie, chips and carrots.

Robson was granted privacy with his client before the interview took place. After only ten minutes he let Ian know they were ready.

Ian went through the procedure with the tapes. Proctor merely looked bored.

It was Barry who began the question and answer session. 'How well did you know the Mercers?'

'Quite well. We'd been neighbours for years.' He was assuming this was still to do with his relationship with Kelly. 'My wife knew them better than me, though, and she got on very well with Dee.'

'And Owen Kerslake?'

'I didn't have a lot to do with him, to be honest. Once he and Dee got together on a permanent basis we didn't see so much of her. They spent every spare minute in each other's company.'

'You obviously knew Kelly well.' Proctor did not respond but, surprisingly, Robson did not step in to advise him not to answer the question. It was unlike him, he was usually as obstructive as the law would permit him to be. Barry let it drop. 'Were you and your wife and Dee Mercer on such terms that you frequently visited each other's houses?'

'Yes. But the women more than myself. We went round there for supper now and again, but not so much since Dee started working at the fish and chip shop and not at all after Owen moved in. Like I said, Eileen used to go round more than me, they'd have coffee and gossip on their days off.'

'And Dee would come round to see your wife in much the same manner?'

'Yes. Usually in the mornings from what Eileen told me.' He stopped and stared at the ceiling before speaking again. He was trying to give the impression that he was being as helpful as possible. 'They'd borrow things sometimes, you know, if they ran out. Neither of them had a car and the nearest shop's a fair walk. But lots of women in Culver Road do that.'

Robson had decided it was time to make his presence felt. 'What's the point of these questions? You already know the answers from your initial interview. My client has admitted to the charges so I really can't see the relevance.'

147

'Maybe not.' Barry gave him one of the grins which he used to believe had women falling at his feet. 'But I can. So, if I may continue?' He turned back to Proctor, who was no longer so relaxed. 'If your family was on such close terms with Dee Mercer there must have been minor disagreements? There usually are between friends, although they're mostly patched up quickly.'

'Disagreements? No, none that I can recall. Dee was a nice woman, I can't imagine anyone falling out with her.'

'But supposing she got to hear of what you were doing with Kelly, your own daughter, that would surely have led to some contention?'

'I don't know what you're trying to do here. I've already made a statement, what more can I do? If you're just trying to make me feel worse, you're wasting your time. She didn't know.'

'How can you be so certain?'

'I should think a child could work that one out. Look, if Dee had any idea she'd have said or done something, she would not have carried on as if nothing had happened.'

'But you just said she hardly came around during the last few years.' Barry saw he was getting to him.

'Don't you listen?' Proctor snapped. 'That was because of Owen.'

'Maybe.'

A small tic appeared at the side of Proctor's face. Barry opened a file in front of him, letting the silence grow. There were five occupants in the small room and the door was closed. It was becoming oppressive and the redolence of the cottage pie lingered in the air. There was no longer any trace of Proctor's aftershave.

Barry looked up and smiled briefly. 'So you had no reason to kill Dee Mercer.' It was a statement, one which caused another silence filled with shock on the part of Proctor and his brief. It even startled Ian, who had not expected him to come out with it so succinctly, but he admired Barry's tactics.

'Kill her? Whatever for? I don't understand what's going on, you've got the man responsible.' He turned to face Robson, who shiftily avoided his eyes. Many thoughts were passing through Robson's sharp mind, not least of which was that he believed the police were having second thoughts about Kerslake's guilt. If he handled this well, gained Proctor's confidence, he might be on his way to handling his first murder case. His speciality was crime but grievous bodily harm was the most serious offence he had so far dealt with. 'I think you ought to answer the questions, Mr Proctor, not confuse the issue with ones of your own.'

Ian could not help but glance at Barry. This was not at all what they had been expecting. About now Robson should have stepped in and demanded a halt to the proceedings or asked for time alone with his client. Ian's eyes narrowed. Of course. He suddenly saw what Robson was about. If Kerslake was off the hook Robson had a chance to make a name for himself. It was Ian who asked a second time, 'Did you kill Dee Mercer?'

'No, I did not. I had absolutely no reason to.'

And so it went on for almost another hour. Between them they used every trick at their disposal to try to catch Proctor out in a lie; every question was asked more than once but phrased differently. Not once did Proctor falter and not once did Robson interrupt. Finally they concluded the interview. Robson asked for, and was granted, a few more minutes alone with Proctor.

'I've been building something out of nothing,' Ian admitted when they had taken seats at an empty table in the canteen. They were both in need of tea. 'Much as I detest what he's done to those girls, I can't see Proctor as guilty of murder.'

'Neither can I. Robson can, though, or hopes he is. Mind you, Proctor's own daughter thinks he's capable of it.'

Ian absent-mindedly spooned three sugars into his tea and stirred it. 'Do you think I'm wrong?'

'About Kerslake? I did at first. We all did. I thought it was just one of your . . . well, we had enough evidence to build a case.' The mood the Chief was in, it was safer not to use words like obsession or fixation. But he seemed not to notice the broken sentence because there was a faraway look on his face.

'What I said before, about everyone knowing things they were keeping from each other and us . . . The daughter knew, Dee Mercer knew. I wonder . . . '

149

Before Barry could ask just what it was he was conjecturing about Ian stood up abruptly, leaving his mug of tea untouched, and walked out of the canteen, hurrying to the general office.

Markham arrived minutes later as the Chief was studying a computer screen. 'Ah, just the man I need.' He outlined what he wanted Markham to do, a request which he agreed to carry out in his usual manner, with a complete lack of curiosity. He liked to operate with little information because he was then able to make an unbiased judgement of whatever situation he found himself in.

Back in the incident room Ian checked Proctor's alibi for the day of the murder. There were no discrepancies. He had hoped that Proctor's job in insurance might have taken him out of the office but he was too high up in the system to be making cold calls or out selling. During the course of the year he was called upon to entertain clients or to be wined and dined by firms of solicitors who handled their personal injury claims, but not so that day. Proctor had spent the whole day in the office, including his lunch break, and this had been corroborated by at least a dozen people. There was no way round it. Proctor had left for work before the time Dee was last seen alive. Other staff confirmed he was there at his usual time and did not leave until four forty-five, earlier than most but he was inclined to arrive early.

'Well, I think I'll pop along to the Crown. Any other takers?' The working day was at an end. Word had got around that the Chief and Barry had failed to make any headway with Proctor, yet instead of the expected gruffness, if not bad-tempered silence, DCI Roper was grinning.

Brenda Gibbons checked her watch. She had not realised it was so late. 'Yes, why not,' she replied. Barry nodded and patted his jacket pocket, checking for cigarettes and keys, and Alan Campbell said he would join them for one but he was going out. Glances were exchanged. Was it possible that their dour, often humourless Scotsman had a date?

'Give me two minutes,' Brenda requested and they watched her sway down the corridor towards the ladies' cloakroom where some of her personal items were in her locker. When

150

she returned she had brushed her hair, leaving it loose, put on fresh lipstick and a rose pink linen jacket which should have clashed with her red skirt but did not.

The four of them strolled up the High Street and down the alleyway which was a short cut to the Crown, a pub situated on the edge of the Green which had been the original hamlet. There was a cloudless sky and more than a hint of the summer to come.

'May I ask why you are looking so smug?' Brenda ventured once they had their drinks in front of them. Bob Jones was at the other end of the bar, polishing steaming glasses as he took them from the machine.

'No particular reason, just something I thought I might follow up.'

'And I thought we were supposed to be a team.'

Ian knew she was right but he felt he might be making a fool of himself if he persisted in believing in Kerslake's innocence. The man had confessed, the evidence pointed to him and he had not been seen during a crucial time when Dee Mercer might have met her death. 'Are you still seeing whatshisname?' he asked to change the conversation.

'Yes, I am, actually.' It was Brenda's turn not to want to discuss the subject. She looked away and pretended to study the price list pinned to the beam beside her. It was going to be a fun evening if every topic they picked was taboo. She might as well go for the hat-trick. 'Where're you going tonight, Alan?'

His white freckled skin turned a strange shade of pink across his prominent cheekbones. 'To the cinema.'

She could not resist it. 'With anyone we know?'

All three were watching him avidly. 'Judy Robbins.' The response was not what Alan had expected. Barry lit a cigarette, Ian nodded and Brenda simply said 'Oh' in a resigned tone. They all knew Judy. This was no date in the real sense of the word. She often spent the evening in the company of a fellow officer but it was only for company, a platonic experience. They wondered if Alan realised this or was hoping for something more. At least Judy was worth the price of a cinema seat – if anyone could make Alan laugh, she would.

151

'Oh, have you heard the news?' Barry took up the conversation. 'The Super's about to become a grandfather.' At one time this would have meant nothing to Barry, but with Lucy two months into her second pregnancy such matters were now of interest to him.

'He doesn't look old enough,' Brenda said.

'He's well into his forties and he had his own family quite young.' Ian had spoken to Mike Thorne many times and not all of their chats concerned work.

'How would you feel?' Barry was aware that Mark was of an age where it was not impossible.

'Difficult to say. Old, I suppose. But proud too. What does the Super think about it?'

'No idea. It was Judy who told me. Alan just reminded me by mentioning her name.'

There was no need to elucidate. For some unknown reason it was always Judy Robbins who heard the news first no matter which rank it involved. Perhaps it was her ability to listen without interruption and to read between the lines which made her the confidante of many.

Ian drank a second pint of Adnam's then surprised them all once more by announcing he was going back to the station. There was no reason to and when he was in the mood for a drink it took something important to make him forgo it. 'See you all tomorrow,' he said cheerfully as he raised a hand to Bob Jones who was in the middle of serving a customer.

As he had hoped, Markham had returned from Culver Road. 'It's possible, sir. I was just going through the file to see who was in that morning.'

'I'll give you a hand. Are these all the statements?'

'Yes.'

'Closest neighbours first, then.'

Together they checked who had been where on the morning of Dee's murder. Several people had been out, the most relevant ones living at numbers 11 and 15. All the occupants had been either at work or at school. Which only left number 13. 'No superstition there,' Ian commented as he read what Mrs Veal had to say. He almost knew the statements by heart but now he was approaching things from a different angle it might be possible to discover they had missed something. Mrs Veal had returned from Rickenham General where she worked as a receptionist on casualty three nights a week. She had made a bacon sandwich and a cup of tea, done a small pile of ironing then taken herself to bed at ten. She had slept until three, or a little after, which was as much as she managed on night shift, then got up again. Her bedroom was at the front of the house and the first she knew that anything was wrong was when she had seen the police cars arriving.

'Could just be,' Ian muttered turning his attention to the plan of the street. The red-brick houses were built in pairs. Each had a small front garden and a larger one at the rear. Running the length of the backs of the houses was a path giving access to the gardens and along which the occupants could wheel their dustbins to the pick-up point on collection day. This path could only be seen from the upstairs windows of adjacent properties because a six foot high wooden slatted fence lent privacy to the gardens and kitchens which were at the back. Ian had asked Markham to walk along this path paying special attention to what he could or could not see from it and also to ask the neighbours, including the family in number 7, if he might take a look from one of the back bedrooms.

'It would be taking a chance,' Markham said, 'but it could be done. Keeping up close to the fence it would be difficult for anyone to see you. And if, as we believe, this was not premeditated, no precautions would have been taken one way. It all makes sense, apart from the dabs. How do you get around that one?'

'I think I know that, Markham, I really think I do.'

'So what now?'

'Now we find out if I'm right.'

'Now?'

Ian thought about it. 'No. It'll keep until the morning, I think that might be best.'

'Yes, sir.' Markham did not ask why; he knew exactly why the Chief had come to that decision.

11

Ian wanted to get the timing right. He believed that was important if his questioning was to make enough impact. As he drove to work he was thinking about Mark, who had rung late the previous night. He was still unable to figure out where he had acquired his artistic ability; no, talent, he amended, his son was more than competent. Now in his final year at Falmouth School of Arts he had made up his mind to go to France in the summer. He had been before, to study the impressionists, but only for two weeks. This time he intended staying for at least a year. He had taken the advice of one of his tutors and Ian hoped he would not regret it. Moira had said she would miss him but that they could pop over for the occasional weekend. Ian had not wished to dampen her enthusiasm by pointing out that under no circumstances would he use the Channel Tunnel, the boat made him sick and he would only fly as a last resort. However, there was nothing to stop Moira going and she could take Philippa, her mother, who was an inveterate traveller and who spoke fluent French. Moira's was almost as good. Ian believed he should be able to make himself understood in English wherever he went and had been accused of being a xenophobe. All this was in the future, not the distant future but far enough away not to have to think about it. For the moment there were other priorities.

Ian waited until Sean Proctor had been driven to the magistrates' court. He was certain it would be a routine hearing; he would be given bail and the case set aside for sentencing when Proctor's lawyer could present any mitigating circumstances. Not that Ian could think of any. In Proctor's absence he sent Sergeant Swan and Constable Gibbons to 17 Culver Road. They were to bring Eileen Proctor in for questioning.

Eileen had spent an uncomfortable and sleepless night on the settee. It was bad enough that Sean had been charged but it seemed that she had lost her daughter too. Everything she had done in her life had been for her family and now they had been rent apart. She could not imagine what a prison sentence would do to Sean. Her only dream had been to keep them together, as a unit, to make things different from her own childhood where the rows had predominated to such an extent that her mother had finally walked out leaving her and her two younger brothers in the care of a worn-out, bad-tempered father. It was Eileen who had taken over her mother's role.

Fear gnawed at her stomach and made her feel nauseous. Numerous times she made a pot of tea, poured a cup and when it was cold took it back to the kitchen and poured it down the sink. 'They can't believe *he* did it,' she kept saying. But Ann, her own daughter, had suggested to the police that Sean might be guilty of worse things than he had already been charged with. Yet the police did make mistakes. They had arrested Owen Kerslake after all, and they were wrong about him.

Eileen had not wanted to go to the court with her husband. She did not want him to be further humiliated by her presence but she was also afraid she might break down and make a scene. She guessed that he would be granted bail; her duty was to wait at home and provide him with a loving welcome when he returned. She must make it clear that she would stand by him no matter what. He needed that much comfort; no one else would want to know him now.

When the door bell rang Eileen jumped but got up quickly to answer it. Sean was earlier than she had expected but, thinking back to newspaper items she had read, she realised he would only have had to give his name and a few personal details and hear the charges read. He must have been the first to appear because it was only ten fifteen.

Her heart sank when she saw who her visitors were. Surely he had not been refused bail?

It was Brenda who spoke. 'Mrs Proctor, I'm Detective Constable Gibbons, we've met before. This is Detective Sergeant Swan. We'd like to ask you some questions and we'd prefer it

155

if you agreed to come with us to the station. We have a car, we can drive you there.' Brenda was studying her closely for a reaction but there did not seem to be one. She looked dreadful; her hair was unbrushed and she probably had not slept. 'Perhaps you'd like to get your bag and a coat?' It wasn't cold but Eileen Proctor was shivering.

'No. I'll be all right like this.' She pulled her cardigan tightly around her as if for protection but raised no objections to going with them. Even though she had been in her clothes all night her skirt hung well because it was lined and her checked Vyella shirt contained the same shade of heather. 'I'll get my bag though.'

Of course, she thought. How stupid of me not to have realised they'd want to talk to me as well. They would need to know if she had known – if she was, she supposed, an accessory. 'I'm ready.' She shut the front door behind her, realising that if it had been Sean he would have let himself in; he had his own key.

She walked between Brenda and Barry to the car which was waiting a few yards down the road. It was unmarked and for that she was grateful. Brenda held the nearside back door open and placed a hand just above Eileen's head as she bent to get in. They were taking no chances. Brenda got in beside her leaving Barry to do the driving. The silence was not broken once in the sixteen minutes it took to reach the station. Eileen stared wordlessly ahead at the back of Barry's head and Brenda, aware that their passenger was tense, sprung as tightly as a coil, even though they were not touching, saw little of what was going on outside the car.

It was Saturday morning and the streets were busy. Barry drove automatically which gave him time to notice traffic and pedestrians alike. He had always dressed in the latest fashions, but smartly, even as a youth. Now he was aware of the varied assortment of clothing people chose to wear. Although it was hardly high summer teenagers were attired in baggy shorts over which they wore equally baggy long shirts or jumpers. On their feet were built-up trainers, the size out of proportion to their legs giving boys and girls alike the appearance of Disney characters. The more conservative were abiding by the adage of ne'er casting a clout as hooded jackets, anoraks and jumpers were also much in evidence.

Eileen Proctor started when they reached their destination, as if she had been unaware where they were going. Barry pulled up outside the main doors to allow his passengers to alight then drove off to park.

Brenda escorted Eileen across the reception area and down the corridor to the interview room where her husband had sat the previous day. On the way she asked for a tray of tea for three to be sent in.

It was the Chief, not Barry, who joined them several minutes later at the same time as the tea arrived. 'I'll leave this to you,' he said quietly as the cups were handed around.

Brenda felt a small jolt of pleasure. A few months ago, in the presence of the DCI, she had been terrified of saying the wrong thing, of getting it altogether wrong. Now her confidence had grown; she had learned different techniques by watching and listening, and knew when to change tack if a line of questioning was getting her nowhere.

Eileen sat quietly, her hands in her lap. There was a blank expression on her face and her exhaustion was apparent but she showed no signs of guilt.

Ian noticed the contrast in the two women. Eileen was care-worn and depressed. Her hair was rather untidy and she gave off a faintly musty smell as if she had not washed recently. On the other hand Brenda was alert, glowing with health and anticipation, and wearing a simple wool dress which showed every curve of her body. From three feet away Ian caught a whiff of her light floral scent. He nodded imperceptibly as a sign for Brenda to begin.

'Mrs Proctor, your husband appeared before the magistrates this morning. Have you any idea why this was?'

'Yes. He told me.'

'I see. How long have you known?'

'Only since he rang me.'

'Since he rang you when?'

'Yesterday. Yesterday after he was arrested.'

Ian waited but, sensibly, Brenda did not pursue the point. They both realised that was the first lie.

157

'And how do you feel about it? I imagine you must be very hurt and angry.'

'I don't know. I haven't had a chance to take it in yet.' She looked up and Brenda saw the pleading expression in her eyes. 'What will happen to him?'

'That will be up to the court to decide. How well did you know Dee Mercer?' She was not going to get involved in a debate about Eileen's husband.

'Very well. She was my friend.'

'And how would you define that friendship, Eileen?'

'I don't understand what you mean.'

'Let me put it this way: we often describe people as our friends when really they're no more than acquaintances, acquaintances that we may see every day, but nonetheless not friends. Friendship entails more than that, it requires trust and confidences and caring. Was that how it was between you and Dee?'

'I see what you mean. Yes, I think we were real friends. We'd go shopping together and had coffee in each other's houses, and meals sometimes, although not so often when she met Owen. When the children were small we'd help each other out. Yes, we were friends.' None of this deviated from what Sean Proctor had told them.

'Thank you. Now I know you've been asked this before, but can you think of any reason why anyone would wish to harm your friend?'

Clever, Ian thought, emphasising the use of the word friend.

'No. Everyone liked her.'

'Did you know that Kelly Mercer was one of the girls your husband has been charged with having an unlawful relationship with?'

Ian gave her another mental Brownie point. They had both witnessed Eileen's reaction; the rapid blinking and the slight involuntary jerk as she was startled by the abrupt change of direction.

'No, Sean didn't say.' But her knuckles were white now as her hands were clasped tightly together.

Brenda paused for a second and studied her own rounded fingernails, which were covered in a pale gloss. The second

158

lie. She had no proof this time but she was certain of it. Mrs Proctor could not be proud of the fact that she had known what was going on and done nothing to prevent it, especially if one of the girls involved was the daughter of a friend and had spent many hours under her own roof. Or were there, as the Chief suspected, other reasons for denying it?

'How did you feel when you heard Dee had been murdered?'

'I was stunned.'

'Only stunned? Surely you felt more than that? She was your friend, after all.'

'Of course I did. But not at once. It was too much to take in. It's only now I've started to realise I'll never see her again.'

'And Kelly, what did you make of it when she disappeared three years ago?'

'I didn't know what to think.' Eileen was becoming agitated. The questions seemed to be going from one thing to another. 'Ann didn't know anything about it. She was just as surprised. We thought she was staying on at school. Dee didn't mention anything either.'

'And you didn't ask? I should've thought you'd be interested in what had happened to her.'

'I did ask. More than once. Dee said that Kelly had changed her mind about her career and had found herself a job and somewhere to live elsewhere.'

'Did you ask where?'

'Yes. I loved that girl. She'd been in and out of my house since the day she could walk. She was like a sister to Ann at one time.'

'What did Dee say?'

'She said Kelly was in temporary accommodation and she'd let me have an address when she'd finally settled. She never did, she just kept avoiding an answer. As time went on I realised Kelly wasn't interested in her old friends.'

Brenda sipped her tea, which was now almost cold. She was beginning to feel she was losing it. She needed to have Eileen Proctor back in the palm of her hand. 'Didn't you find it odd that Dee never even mentioned the town or city Kelly was living in?'

'Not at first. She was so natural about it it didn't cross my mind. I thought Kelly might have changed. She was a wonderful little girl but she might have become a bit snobbish.'

'All right. But I'm surprised, if you were so fond of the girl, that you didn't press the point. You didn't, did you?'

Ian could not see where this was leading. He hoped he hadn't misjudged Brenda's abilities. Seconds later he saw he had not.

'No. I didn't.' Eileen's tone was almost defiant.

'Why not?'

'I don't know.'

'Could it be that you *did* know about your husband and Kelly? Was it because you'd guessed Dee had sent her away, out of danger, and if you pressed the point you might discover your husband's crime was no secret?'

The crimson flush which spread upwards from Eileen Proctor's neck was answer enough. Brenda repeated the question. 'Did you know?'

Eileen exhaled. It was half a sob. 'Yes. All right then. I did know. Are you happy now?'

'That was three years ago.'

'I . . .' Eileen stopped. Too late she had seen the trap. She recalled her brief telephone call with Sean of the previous day. He had simply told her he had been arrested and that she was not to worry. Naturally he would not have been allowed to make that call in private in case he tried to arrange an alibi or get her to lie for him. They had known that, had known exactly what he said to her. She could not get out of it now. 'I love my husband. I knew if I said anything he might go to prison.'

Brenda was aware of the lengths to which certain women would go to protect the men they loved, or those they feared, no matter what their actions. 'But you were prepared to let it carry on. Didn't you ever give any thought to the children involved and what they might be going through?'

Eileen's anguish was plain but they could not stop now. 'He didn't hurt them,' she said, 'and I'm quite sure they were willing.' It was an excuse, one she had been making to herself for years, one she had needed to make if she was to live with it.

160

'What makes you say that?' Brenda wondered if the Proctor relationship was so bizarre that they actually discussed it.

Eileen mumbled something which Brenda asked her to repeat.

'I said she looked like she was smiling in the photograph.'

'Who was?'

'Kelly.'

'You've seen photographs of Kelly?' Brenda could not keep the surprise out of her voice. 'Where were these photographs?'

'In Sean's briefcase. They're not there now, it was a couple of years ago.'

It was likely that once the girl had moved away he had had the sense to destroy them. 'When Kelly left did your husband ask why she'd gone? Did he, in fact, mention her at all?'

'No. Not once. Oh, except he said he was glad that Ann hadn't decided to leave home. He wanted her to stay with us until she was married.'

'I have to ask you this, Eileen, did you ever have any suspicions that your husband might have interfered with your daughter in any way?'

'No. Never!' She was adamant. 'Sean's always been a good father.'

'All right, just a couple more questions. What were your movements on the day that Dee Mercer was killed?'

'I've already told you that.'

'I know, but we'd like to run through them again.' Brenda was very much aware of the Chief to her left. His feet were planted firmly on the ground and his arms were folded across his chest. She could not guess from his posture or the closed expression on his face how he was judging her interviewing technique but she was not receiving any bad vibes and he had not interrupted her.

Eileen Proctor sighed. 'I got Sean and Ann up. I always take them a cup of tea. Sean went off to work then Ann left about half an hour later. She starts at eight but she likes to walk in because she's sitting behind that check-out most days. I cleared up the breakfast things then went into town myself about nine o'clock. It's about a twenty-minute walk. I got the

161

week's groceries and came home in a taxi. We don't have a second car.'

'If you work in the supermarket wouldn't it be easier to get what you want each day? I assume you get a staff discount either way?'

'We do, but I prefer doing it all at once. It's less hassle and I don't forget things.'

Brenda did not agree but it was not a crime. 'And then?'

'The taxi dropped me at the door, I suppose it was about ten fifty, eleven o'clock. They always come pretty quickly, there's a free-phone number in the supermarket. I unpacked the food then I put another load of washing in the machine.' There had been the slightest hesitation as Eileen spoke, as if she might have done something in between these two activities. 'Then, like I do every day off, I cleaned the house from top to bottom. I had a break about one then finished off the downstairs. After that I had a cup of tea and read a magazine until it was time to get the supper on.'

'When you're cleaning, in the bathroom, for instance, do you wear rubber gloves?'

Eileen was puzzled. 'Yes. Most women do.'

Ian gave a small nod of satisfaction. He saw where Brenda was heading; the girl would go far.

'On the day Dee was murdered did you, by any chance, forget something? You say you shop in one go, perhaps there was one item you didn't pick up?'

They both noticed the flicker of Eileen's heavy eyelids, a sign that the question had thrown her. 'No.'

'You're sure?'

'Of course I'm sure. I'd just been to the shops, I always take a list, and cross things off as I go.'

Brenda chewed her lip. How convenient it would have been if she had forgotten soap powder or bath cleaner. It had been a hunch, no more than that, and it would have explained that although Eileen's fingerprints were in the house, as was to be expected, there were none on the door handle or the knife. If she'd popped along in her rubber gloves for a squirt of Jif, say, they'd be home and dry. Then she saw her mistake. If it had been that way there would have been no need to wash the knife, not if her hands were covered. 'Thank you, Eileen, we'll take a break now.' She dictated the time of the end of the first part of the interview, switched off the tape, removed it and sealed it before she and Ian left the room. A WPC was sent in to keep Eileen company.

'Why break off there? You were getting to her.'

'I know, but there's something I want to check before we continue.'

'Are you going to enlighten me?'

Brenda grinned. 'I thought you'd have guessed by now.'

Ian followed her down the corridor, his hands in his pockets. 'I suspect you want to look at the pictures again.'

She turned around, still smiling. 'You've got it in one.' They made their way to the large room where the copy of the file which had been sent to the DPP's office was kept.

'She wasn't lying, not when she said she didn't borrow anything, but the question still upset her.'

'Quite. But she could have gone to number 9 for another reason.'

The scene-of-crime team had been as meticulous as ever and the photographers had taken numerous shots from every conceivable angle both of the body and of the kitchen itself. They ignored the ones of Dee and concentrated on the others. Apart from the blood they included everything you would expect to see in a family kitchen. They flicked quickly through the prints at first then both stopped and raised their heads at the same time. It proved nothing, but there was a chance they were right. On the draining board was a full jar of paprika.

'A jar,' Brenda commented, 'not one of the refill packets. She was cutting up beef, she must have been going to make a goulash or something similar.' Through a magnifying glass they were able to ascertain that the plastic pull-off seal was still intact. They stood in silence. It was, of course, mere speculation, there was nothing to say that Dee had not purchased it herself.

'Get out the sheet with the list of Dee's telephone calls.' Brenda did so. 'As I thought,' Ian said. 'Look, eight thirty-five. Dee rang Eileen. Was the jar checked for dabs?'

'I would imagine so.' Brenda rummaged around until she

163

found the report. 'It was. They've only got one definite, and that was Dee's, everything else is inconclusive. Lots of people would've handled that jar. Do I go back and take a chance, sir?'

'Yes.'

Eileen Proctor was sipping tea but she had not touched the biscuits. In their absence she seemed to have shrunk.

'Right. You say that you didn't run out of anything on the morning of Dee's death, but let's put it the other way. Dee asked you to pick something up for her, didn't she?'

'I . . . No.' Eileen shook her head.

'Paprika. We found the jar. She rang you and asked you to get it for her because she needed it that day. It had the same supermarket sticker.'

'Dee shopped there too.'

'Not that day. You took it to her and you quarrelled. Over Sean maybe, or over Kelly, then in a fit of temper you killed her. You're taller than Dee and stronger and the knife was lying there. And then you let Owen Kerslake take the blame. Just as you continued to allow your husband to have sex with young girls.'

'Oh, God.' Eileen slumped forward in an attitude of complete defeat.

'The jar's been sent for analysis. The results will show whether or not you handled it, Mrs Proctor.'

And then it was over. Eileen rocked back and forth sobbing. 'I did it,' she finally gasped. 'I didn't mean to, I really didn't mean to. It was all for Sean. Everything I've ever done's been for him. I couldn't bear it, you see, not when she told me.'

'Slow down, Mrs Proctor, let's take it one step at a time. You went to the supermarket and when you returned you went around to give Dee the spices.'

Very slowly the story came out. Along with it came her avowals of love for her husband and child and how she had sworn nothing would ever get in the way of the family. They listened, not unaffected, but not shocked. They had seen it all before.

Eileen had returned from the shops and done a few chores before remembering that Dee needed the paprika that morning and going down the back alley to her house. As far as she

164

was aware no one had seen her. She had been invited to stay for coffee but before it was made the row had started. It was an argument which became ridiculously out of hand, one that finally sent a woman who had been living on her nerves for all of her married life over the edge.

'I always suspected, you know, but without proof it didn't seem to matter. I loved Sean. Then I found the photographs. I was upset but as long as no one else knew it didn't seem to matter. When Dee told me what she knew it was the end. I was talking about Sean, you see, praising him. Dee gave me a funny look and I asked what she meant by it. She said something about not being too sure that he was so wonderful.'

Eileen continued for several minutes. Her account of the row was disjointed but it appeared that she'd riled Dee to the point where Dee blurted out that she knew about the girls and that Kelly had also been involved.

'I didn't believe her, not at first. Not when she said Sean was Kelly's father. She was too old. Then I realised that she wouldn't have been at the time. That she's younger than me. I had to stop her. You must understand I had to shut her up. I went for the knife. I only meant to frighten her. She just looked at me. She said I ought to go to the police and that if I didn't she would, regardless of the consequences to Kelly.'

There was a pause. Eileen began sobbing again. When she was calmer she continued. 'I stabbed her. I only meant to frighten her. When I saw what I'd done I knew we'd both be in trouble. I couldn't stop myself. I kept on stabbing her. It was for Sean, I did it for Sean.'

'And afterwards?'

'I was quite calm. I remember being surprised how calm I was. I put on Dee's rubber gloves and washed the knife. I'd got my overall on. There was blood all over it but it was patterned. I took it off anyway in case anyone saw me. When I got back I had a bath and washed my clothes. I wrapped the overall and my shoes in a bag and put it in the bin. It didn't seem to matter now that Sean was out of danger.'

'And you carried on as normal?'

'It wasn't hard, not after what I'd been through.'

They went over it all several times. There was no doubt of

Eileen's guilt. She made a statement and signed it. She, too, had nothing left to live for. Her main concern now centred upon her daughter. At least Ann had Richie. She would need him with both parents serving prison sentences.

As they left the interview room Ian thought the psychiatrists would have a field day with the Proctors.

12

They were celebrating in the Feathers when Ian remembered to ask how Lucy's appointment at the clinic had gone.

'She's fine. She's had a scan and everything's all right. We were allowed to keep the negatives. I can't believe it, you can actually make out the baby's shape. Bloody amazing.'

Markham winked at Brenda. Here was the cool Barry Swan animated about his wife's pregnancy. They hoped he wasn't going to produce the negative. It was hard to imagine what he'd be like once the child was born. 'It must be a weight off your mind,' Brenda was kind enough to say, at the risk of hearing more about the embryo. As she turned to speak Andrew Osborne entered the pub and she felt her cheeks redden. He would not join her, not whilst she was with her colleagues, but he raised a hand in greeting and smiled at her fondly. They were meeting again the following evening. So far the relationship had remained platonic, not even a goodnight kiss, for which she was grateful. They were getting to know one another and now she was starting to hope it would not remain that way. Andrew moved to the end of the bar and joined a colleague of his own.

'You were right all along,' Barry was saying to Ian, not having noticed the small interaction between Brenda and Andrew. 'And Kerslake will be released.'

'Yep. He's got a case for wrongful arrest if he decides to follow it up, but somehow I doubt it.'

'I agree.' Markham had spoken to him. 'He's devastated, he doesn't seem to care about anything except that he won't be seeing Dee again. There's a chance he might change his mind later.'

'What's he going to do? Barry inquired.

'He's got no plans long term. For the time being he's going to find some cheap bed and breakfast in London, near Kelly. She was delighted, by all accounts, and I suppose it's some recompense.'

'What about Proctor? Isn't she worried about him any more?'

'No. Now that she knows he didn't kill her mother. Also she's realised she's too old for his tastes now. Your round, I believe, Chief?'

'Again? It can't be.'

Nobody commented upon the little charade which was acted out every time they had a drink; no one pointed out that the 'again' was superfluous as Ian had not bought one at all. He sighed dramatically and reached into his jacket pocket for his wallet. He felt shattered but justified. This time there were no doubts, this time the DPP could not fail to be satisfied. Not only had Eileen confessed but she had provided details only the murderer could know. Superintendent Thorne was satisfied too. He had harboured his own doubts, despite Kerslake's confession and the lies he had told. All that remained for them to complete was the paperwork. Not so for the others involved. The Proctor family was no more and nothing would ever be the same again for Kelly or Owen Kerslake. Michelle Short and Lizzie Conrad, though, would no longer have anything to fear. Their past mistakes had come to light but would not interfere with their futures.

It was late when they disbanded and it had been dark for some time. Ian stepped out on to the pavement and breathed in air that was cleaner than in the pub. The sky was clear but no stars were visible because they were masked by the glow of the lights of Rickenham Green. He walked slowly home, passing a group of youths who eyed him aggressively. His anger rose. If anything happened he would not hesitate to have a go, but supposing he was a female? He doubted if he'd ever go out alone at night. There was no end to it, not now. They might have cleared up two crimes but it was the tip of the iceberg. It was, he realised, also his *raison d'être*.

Disco music and flashing lights emanated from the Black Horse where the landlord had picked up most of the rough trade from the Prince William once that had become a gay bar. Ian turned into a side road similar to Belmont Terrace. The traffic noise lessened and soon he was almost at his front door. Curtains were drawn down both sides of the street and some of the houses were unlit. Not so his own. A welcoming semicircle of light showed through the stained glass over the door. Moira was still up. He was pleased.

'It's only me,' he called as he opened the door.

Moira was in the kitchen studying a brochure of sorts. Beside her was half a glass of wine. 'You're later than I expected. Ah, you've been celebrating?'

'Sorry, love. I forgot to ring.'

She shrugged. She was not that concerned and it was rare for him not to let her know.

'Lucy's okay, by the way. She's had a scan.'

'Good. I'm very pleased for her.' Her eyes returned to the brochure.

'What's that you're reading?'

'I've been thinking, I don't have many hobbies, apart from gardening and dressmaking, I thought I'd go to evening classes when the next term begins. I picked this up in the library.'

Ian pulled out a chair and sat down; under the fluorescent tube Moira saw how tired he was. 'You were right, weren't you?'

He nodded.

'Well done. I'm very proud of you.'

'Stick the kettle on, will you? I could really fancy a cup of tea.'

If he had not been so tired she would have told him to do so himself. 'What happens now?'

'Kerslake goes free.'

'Is he going to make a complaint?'

'We don't think so.'

'I'm sorry. You don't need me asking a load of questions.'

168

'I'd like to talk about it. If you're not too tired.'

'No. Carry on.'

Ian waited until a pint mug of tea was in front of him. It was peaceful in the kitchen; the light buzzing overhead, the fridge humming before switching itself off again and his wife opposite him. 'Where would you draw the line?' Ian asked.

Moira refilled her glass. She suspected they would not be going to bed for at least another hour. 'In what way?'

'If I'd done something you knew was wrong, how far would you go to protect me?'

'Goodness, Ian, that's bit deep for this time of night.' She placed an elbow on the table and a finger against her lips as she thought. 'I suppose it would depend what it was.'

'Ah, so there are degrees of wrong, are there?'

'Yes, to me there are. I know you don't think like that but you see everything in terms of black and white.'

'You'd break the law to protect me?'

'Yes. In certain circumstances, I think I would.'

'Women are far more devious than men, you know.' Moira ignored that. 'Would you kill to protect me?'

'Oh no.' She smiled and shook back her shoulder-length fair hair. 'Not even I'd stoop that far.'

'Eileen Proctor did.'

A cool breeze from the partly open window stirred the pages of the brochure Moira had been studying. Ian nodded towards it. 'Decided what you want to do yet?'

'Not really.'

'I can't see you arranging flowers or getting a fix on sugar-craft.'

'Neither can I.' She chewed the end of her pen. 'I was thinking more along the lines of a language or A level law.'

Ian slapped his forehead dramatically. 'No, no. Please preserve me from that.'

Moira shrugged. Why not law? She could already speak French and they did not take that many foreign holidays. Ian had made up her mind for her. 'Law it is.'

'Well, I suppose if the lovely Brenda Gibbons can make a go of it with the enemy, I suppose I could live with a woman with a qualification in the subject.'

'Brenda's got a boyfriend?'

'Yes. One Andrew Osborne.'

'Do I know him?'

'I think so. Tall bloke, pock-marked. Ugly creature.'

'Ah, I know who you mean. Ugly? Do you think so? I find him rather attractive myself.'

It was not the first time Ian had been amazed at what women found attractive and, looking at Moira, he was more than grateful for the fact. 'Come on, let's go up.' He closed the window, checked the doors and switched off the lights.

As he lay in bed he gave a thought to the characters he had recently met and come to know better than he knew some of his colleagues. And they, despite all the awfulness and all the dirt with which they came into contact, managed to live their own lives regardless. There was Barry Swan, married and about to become a father, Judy Robbins recovering from the loss of her father and Brenda Gibbons apparently making a new start. And Markham. Ian's lips twitched in a sleepy smile. What was there to say about Markham? And in a fortnight Barry would sit his final inspector's exam. If he passed Ian would lose him, and he did not want to do that. As he drifted into sleep he wasn't sure if he wanted Barry to pass.